I Still Ride For My Hitta

Misty Holt

**Lock Down Publications
& Ca$h Presents
I Still Ride For My Hitta
A Novel by *Misty Holt***

Misty Holt

Lock Down Publications

P.O. Box 1482

Pine Lake, Ga 30072-1482

Visit our website at **www.lockdownpublications.com**

First Edition February 2017

Printed in the United States of America

This is a work of fiction. Names, characters, places, and incidents either are products of the author's imagination or are used fictitiously. Any similarity to actual events or locales or persons, living or dead, is entirely coincidental.

Cover design and layout by: Dynasty's Cover Me

Book interior design by: Shawn Walker

Edited by: Mia Rucker

Stay Connected with Us!

Text **LOCKDOWN** to 22828 to stay up-to-date with new releases, sneak peaks, contests and more…

Submission Guideline.

Submit the first three chapters of your completed manuscript to ldpsubmissions@gmail.com, subject line: Your book's title. The manuscript must be in a .doc file and sent as an attachment. Document should be in Times New Roman, double spaced and in size 12 font. Also, provide your synopsis and full contact information. If sending multiple submissions, they must each be in a separate email.

Have a story but no way to send it electronically? You can still submit to LDP/Ca$h Presents. Send in the first three chapters, written or typed, of your completed manuscript to:

LDP: Submissions Dept
Po Box 1482
Pine Lake, Ga 30072

DO NOT send original manuscript. Must be a duplicate.

Provide your synopsis and a cover letter containing your full contact information.

Thanks for considering LDP and Ca$h Presents.

Acknowledgements

LDP Stand Up!! The support and love that goes around our family is like no other! I love you all! #TheGameIsOurs

To My Girls... Anything I do is for you two. I can't imagine life without you ladies. Y'all make me smile and dry my tears when it's necessary. You cheer me on. You give me hope. I only ask one thing... Always remain yourselves.

Boo... You already know what it is, so I'll just say thank you and I love you, baby.

Shawn/Coffee... The only thing I hate about our friendship is that we waited so long to spark it up. It doesn't matter what time of day or night I pop in your inbox, you will have an answer. I've said it once I'll say it a million more... You are so important to all of our success. I admire you so much. Keep doing your thing, Queen.

To My Other Mother: We aren't even blood but you're the only one in my family who has been supportive. I love you even more for that. Thanks, Ma.

To my Daddy: Not a day goes by that I don't miss you. Not a day goes by that I don't crack a smile and shed a tear thinking about something you said or did. You made me who I am. I love you, daddy. S.I.P

Ca$h... You pushed me so hard to make this book better and even though I whined pleaded begged and talked ish, I really appreciated it. Thanks, King, for giving us all a platform.

Mandi, Hatter, and LeeLee we did it again ladies!! You know I say we cuz we are a true team. Gosh y'all have seen and comforted me so much. I love y'all.

Readers... Please don't be mad at me. That's all I can say.

Haters... Y'all can go on and hate me!

Chapter One
Ivory

As I sat in the chair across from my best friend, I washed my hand across my face. I just couldn't believe my ace had been laid up in a coma for two weeks behind that hoe ass nigga, Money. Then while me and the crew were turning North Texas on its side looking for *their* missing children, this dude was nowhere to be found. I shook my head as a pounding erupted at my temples. So much had gone on in the last two weeks, it seemed as if I had a never ending migraine.

"Schina, bitch, you gotta shake this shit. Nicole and I still have no idea who has Tai and Liv and your sorry ass husband..." I trailed off trying to find a sensitive way to tell her my thoughts. "Well he ain't shit," I said, deciding not to beat around the bush. "I wanna bust that nigga in his shit, but I'm not sure how bad you gone trip. I know how you get behind his bitch ass."

Two weeks ago, Schina, her husband Money, Nicole and I had been enjoying a peaceful vacation on Jorge, our new connect's, massive estate when I received a hysterical call from Schina's daughters' and my goddaughters' nanny. *"Ms. Ivory,"* and then all I heard was a slew of jumbled words. It was so bad, I had to make her start over.

"Ms. Thomas, I need you to calm down. Take a couple of deep breaths and then start over."

I realized immediately, if she was calling on me, it had to be something bad. I pushed my chair out, causing a terrible screeching sound. I could see that it startled Jorge and Nicole by the jerks of their heads. Nicole quickly picked up on my demeanor, causing her to jump up almost as fast as me.

"What is it?" she asked curiously, as she reached for her pistol. I scrunched my face and waved at her to put away her weapon. Not wanting to say much, I just pointed upstairs, where

Schina and Money's suite was located. We began to jog towards her room as I listened to the elder nanny gulp in breaths of air.

Once she seemed to have calmed down, she began her story again. "Schina isn't answering her phone. Y'all need to get to Orlando or Dallas, whichever y'all think is best. But y'all need to do it as soon as possible."

Getting impatient, and tired of my mind conjuring up images of all the things that may have happened, I snapped. "Just tell me what the fuck is going on. Quit beating around the fucking bush." I listened to my voice echo as Nicole stared at me with surprise written all across her face. I'm not normally as crass as Schina, but I needed to know what was going on back home. Why would she say Orlando or Dallas?

"Well I never..." she began before I quickly cut her off.

I let her catch another taste of my disdain as I spat, "And you never fucking will if you don't get to the fucking point, you old bitch." By then I was beyond angry.

I heard the older woman expel a deep breath, but she kept on with her story. I was glad she had seemed to make the right decision. I was ready to wring her old wrinkled up neck.

"When I woke up this morning to get the girls ready to get to the airport, they were missing from their beds."

"What do you mean missing? Well where the fuck are they?" I asked her as Nicole and I rounded another curve of the spiraling staircase.

"There was a note on the dresser. It says do not call the police. You took something I love. Now I have something that you love. Two somethings. Game on bitch."

My mouth dropped open as we finally made it to the massive door of Schina and Money's suite. I noticed, out of the corner of my eye, Jorge was now following behind us as well. To make it even more intense, there were two armed guards bringing up the rear.

I didn't even bother to knock, just flung open the door. "We have to..." I never finished my statement. The sight before me rendered me speechless. As the door slung open, Money was releasing Schina's limp body. I couldn't do anything as I watched her go crashing to the ground.

I was jerked back to the present by a weird hissing sound. I had spent so much time in Schina's expensive ass hospital room, I knew every sound every machine made. Hell, I even knew why. That was a new sound, though. I snatched my head up, peering in Schina's direction.

I rubbed my eyes to make sure I wasn't tripping. I jumped up with excitement when I realized it was really happening. Schina's eyes were open. I rushed to her bedside and pressed the nurse's button as her eyes fluttered open and closed like a newborn after naptime.

"How can I help you?" An almost mechanical voice boomed from somewhere in the chilly room. I had always hated how cold they kept it in hospitals. It was almost like they were prepping you for the morgue.

"Yes, ma'am. Sch... I mean Raschina's eyes are open. She's awake pointing at her neck," I said excitedly. Even though I didn't know who I was praying to, it felt like I had been praying for an eternity.

Just as I was about to get angry because the nurse hadn't responded, the door flew open. It looked like a sea of blue rushed in the room. An older woman walked in my direction with her arms outstretched. "We need you to leave the room. As soon as we have something to tell you, we will be right out. Just have a seat in the waiting room."

Nicole and I had her transported from Mexico to Parkland Trauma Center in Dallas. I knew she was in good hands, but I just didn't want to leave her. After the nurse gave me a reassuring pat, I threw a glance over my shoulder, peeking at my best friend.

As I walked out the door, I passed the two guards Jorge had ordered to watch over our girl. Yea, she was in good hands.

I pulled out my personal phone, a purple blinged out Galaxy S6, and held the two button down. I listened to the steady ringing as I waited for the third in our triumvirate, Nicole, to answer the phone. She hadn't spent much time by Schina's side, and I hoped it was because she had been causing major chaos in the streets. We were leaving no stones unturned in the search for the girls.

"Now's not a good time," Nicole panted breathlessly. I assumed her and Blue had taken a moment to bust a nut or two, even though with him locked up it was only phone sex. But hey, I wasn't mad at 'em. I couldn't even remember the last time I had sex.

"I don't give a damn about your freaky ass sex sessions. You need to get down here. Schina just woke up." I knew I sounded like a hater, but I didn't even care. I needed some dick and it was getting ridiculous. I *had* been talking to Money's boy, Blacc. The same nigga who sent us on the mission to kill my daughter's dad. He was still locked up, but he was set to be released in four days. I couldn't wait. I had plans on putting this pussy all in his life.

I headed to the vending machine in the middle of the waiting room and scanned the selections. I didn't really have an appetite, but I knew I needed something on my stomach. I grabbed a Sprite and some peanut M&Ms. As I turned to take a seat, my business line rang. "Speak to me."

"Someone close to you set this in motion. You need to be careful." The voice ejected from my phone sounded mechanical. I figured they were using a voice scrambler.

"What you talking about, my nigga?" I shot back. I knew no-one in our circle set this up. No-one would have any reason to. I was sure this was a diversion. At least I hoped it was.

"I know y'all think everyone in your little crew is loyal, but that's not the case. Someone in your crew knows where the girls are. They are working with the people who grabbed them. Watch your back."

Before I could utter another word, I heard the call disconnect. I sank into the nearest chair as the call played over and over in my head. It was like a C.D. stuck on repeat.

I must have played it in my head a million times, because the next thing I knew, Nicole was shaking me.

"Bitch, what the fuck is wrong with you?" Her voice was full of exasperation. "I called your name five damn times. Now is not the time for your ass to lose it."

I couldn't do anything but look at her and shake my head. "I just received..." before I could finish my sentence, I saw the same nurse who had escorted me out of Schina's room heading in our direction.

"Oh, that's one of Schina's nurses. Come on. Let's go find out what's going on with our girl." I grabbed Nicole by the sleeve of her long-sleeved T-shirt and started dragging her towards the nurse. I was anxious to find out how my girl was. Schina and I had been to hell and back together, and I loved her like my own mother had birthed her.

Before I had gotten five steps away, Nicole snatched back. "I'm perfectly capable of walking on my own." I noticed what sounded like disgust in her voice. When I thought about it, her attitude lately had been real stank. I didn't have time to deal with it at that moment, but I damn sure made a mental note to address that shit later.

"Well, bitch, bring ya ass." I scurried off leaving Nicole standing in the same place. As I got closer to the nurse, my heartbeat increased as I noticed tears in her big brown eyes. As tears sprang to my own eyes, I managed to open my mouth and utter one word, before I had to stop and lean against the nearest wall. "Please."

"Oh no! I'm so sorry." The nurse's facial expression changed to one of compassion, as she again reached her tiny hands out to me. It crossed my mind that it was amazing she could save lives with such small hands. "Schina is fine. Well, as fine as can be expected. She is indeed awake. There were some issues but the doctors got them taken care of and now she is being taken down for a MRI."

I was no doctor, but I knew MRIs were used to check the brain, so I was even more confused. "What kind of issues? Why an MRI? What's wrong with her brain? When can I see her?"

By then, I was off of the wall and hovering over the nurse. Just as I was about to reach out to grab her, I was snatched from behind.

I had almost forgotten Nicole was even there. "Ivory, give her a chance to tell us what's going on before you turn into a drama queen, shit."

It took everything in me not to turn around and knock the shit out of her ass at that very moment, but I knew I couldn't afford the drama. Instead of clowning, I just turned back to the nurse. I was trying to search her face for answers.

"I know you're worried about Mrs. Morgan. It's just protocol. The doctors just want to make sure her brain waves are normal, and that she is doing okay. She should be back in her room shortly. I give you my word that I will be out to get you as soon as the doctors give the okay. Just sit down and relax as much as possible. She is very lucky not only to be alive but to have a true friend like you Ms. Bettis." With those final words, she kind of cut her eyes at Nicole and sashayed off.

"What did that bitch mean by that? Just because I'm not up here going crazy wit' yo' ass doesn't mean I'm not a good friend. Shit, I just realize there's nothing I can do for her, Tai or Liv sitting in this place. Man, fuck her." Nicole glared at me before stomping off to the hard couches provided in the waiting room.

Usually it was packed on this floor, but today there was no-one here besides Nicole and I. I hadn't decided on if that was a good thing or not. I wasn't sure what was going on with Nicole but I damn sure planned on getting to the bottom of it.

As I headed in her direction, ready to at least tell her about the mysterious call I had received, something made me change my mind. Instead I headed to a seat in the corner. I needed a moment to get my head on right. I knew I couldn't do that messing with Nicole's sometimey ass.

As I thought back to the day Schina brought her bourgeois ass around, I realized I had never grown to love her as Schina had.

"Hey best friend," Schina called as she walked up. She was wearing a short-sleeved t-shirt that read Flawless in silver glitter, a pair of mid-thigh white shorts, and her signature pink flip flops. Her long curly hair had been pulled back by a pink headband and her pink glasses were perched on the tip of her nose. But more noticeable than her outfit was the chic following behind her.

Old girl stood an inch shorter than Schina putting her at five feet seven inches. She looked like she weighed one hundred sixty-five pounds, putting her somewhere between thick and big. Bitch looked like if she had one too many value meals she would go straight to fat, but who was I to talk? I had always been on the heavy side, but I was sexy as fuck with it, though. She had skin the color of early morning coffee with just a dab of cream. Her eyes were a hazel color and seemed to twinkle with mischief.

What really made her stand out was the one piece neon orange short set and white gladiator sandals she was rocking. It was obviously one of those expensive ass outfits, something Schina nor myself would ever be caught in. We just weren't into the latest trends, preferring to be comfortable instead of in style.

"Who the hell is this bitch," *I thought to myself. Schina and I had been rocking solo for two years. She knew I didn't like new people. But every now and then, she would try that shit, though. I had always vetoed the newbie. I had no idea why Schina thought this bitch was going to be any different.*

The new girl must have read my mind. She flipped her long auburn curls over her shoulder and stuck her hand out. "Hey, I'm Nicole. You must be Ivory."

I simply stared at her hand before turning to Schina. "Bitch, I done told you about feeding the strays."

I laughed as I remembered how Schina sighed, and Nicole's face flushed that day. I ended up having to whoop her ass in the parking lot of Dave & Buster's, but surprisingly Nicole still came around.

I decided to try to make nice with Nicole, again, for Schina's sake. "Look, bitch," I said headed in Nicole's direction. "Now isn't the time for us to be tripping. Schina is going to need us, so let's just not kiss, but make up."

"Man, I'm more worried about how we gone tell Schina the girls are still missing. How do we come out and say her husband is a piece of shit? That's what's the most important. Fuck that shit you talking."

I couldn't help but notice she had been typing away at her phone the whole time she was speaking. "Well why don't you get off the damn phone so we can figure out our next move," I said as I continued to walk in her direction.

"Look, Ivory, I'm not in the mood. We have entirely too much going on for you to be on the let's mama Nicole shit," she responded with a voice full of attitude.

I rolled my tired eyes as I sank into the chair nearest her, giving my weary body a chance to rest. I washed my hand across my face again before I tried to muster up a reply. Nicole had always been more sensitive than Schina and I, and we always tended to baby her. I didn't plan on babying her, but I knew not to fully go off on her ass either.

"So, Nicole, how much do you think we should tell her? And how the hell do we tell her?" I never fathomed having to tell Schina we hadn't found the girls. They were her whole life, and my Godchildren. I knew she would expect better of me.

Nicole sighed as she slid her phone in her pocket. "Considering how Schina is, I think we should just give it to her raw and unfiltered." I guess my face showed my doubt because she threw up a long manicured nail and continued on with her statement. "You know if we beat around the bush she's gonna know. And I'm sure you feel she can't handle the whole truth right now, but it's her *kids* we are talking about. If it was Danyelle, you would want to know the truth, right?"

Hearing her speak my daughter's name made me picture my chocolatey chinky-eyed baby. I hadn't seen her in a couple of days and I needed to. I just didn't think it was the right time to bring her back to Texas, considering the mess we were in.

To avoid the depression I knew would settle in, I snapped myself back into reality. I was just in time to see the nurse headed back in our direction.

.

Chapter Two
Money

"Bitch, you got me fucked up." I could feel myself foaming at the mouth, as I tightened my grip around the hoe's neck. *I don't even know her fucking name,* I thought. It was at that exact moment I realized how low I had sank.

I had no idea how my wife was doing. I had no idea who had my kids. Hell, I didn't even know if any of them were alive. The only thing I did know, was if that bitch Ivory got her hands on me, I was one dead ass nigga.

All I remembered about the day my life started fucking up, was receiving that video. The video that showed my wife letting some dike eat what was supposed to be *my* pussy.

I didn't remember anything else until I was rushing past Jorge and the Queens. I knew I needed to get the fuck off that estate.

I later found out, through the streets of course, why Ivory and Nicole were even looking for us. They were trying to tell Schina and I the girls had been snatched from their hotel room. But being real with myself, by the time the news made it to me, I was in another world. One that included nothing but Ciroc, diesel, and pussy.

Ebony, yea, that was the bitch's name, I thought as I snapped back to my current dilemma. I couldn't quite shake the fog in my head. Couldn't even remember why I wanted her dead, so I just let the bitch go.

"It ain't no bitch out here bad enough to get no coins from me, hoe," I said with a voice full of malice. I had finally remembered what the problem was. "If I ain't even at home taking care of my wife, what the fuck make you think you're that special? That's what's wrong with y'all young ass bitches now."

I still couldn't believe this hoe tried to charge me. And then the pussy she threw on me was loose as fuck, too? Fuck that and fuck her, too.

I scanned the cheap ass motel room trying to find my clothes. I had to get the fuck up out of there. As I saw my clothes huddled up in a dark corner of the room, I let my eyes fall on Ebony. I was trying to recall why I had even picked her. She was alright, standing five feet five inches and weighing one hundred fifteen pounds. She was more slender than what I usually gravitated towards. She had skin the color of molasses and natural grey eyes.

But that was where the natural ended. She rocked a waist length weave that at one point was curly and pretty. By then it just looked like a bird nest. She had started out the night with perfectly applied makeup. Even that had begun to look clownish. She had a small waist and it barely seemed to support the ass shots she had to 'enhance' her ass. Those were her words not mine. She sported long purple acrylic nails. I was willing to bet my car that the long purple toenails she had scratched my leg with, were fake too. I couldn't do anything but shake my head. I was feeling so disappointed in myself.

I refused to look in the mirror as I quickly threw on the True Religion jeans and t-shirt I had started the evening in. I hadn't had a hair cut or shaved my face in days. I had even overheard a member of the crew comment to another member I looked like I was on that shit.

As I grabbed my keys, I thought of the situation with Bianca. The situation that started this whole downward spiral. I quickly surmised it would be cheaper to just drop the hoe some money. As I hit the door, I pulled five twenty dollar bills from my pocket and threw them in her general direction. I didn't even care that she hadn't uttered another word. She just sat in the same spot I had dropped her. She would throw looks in my direction but never gave eye contact.

"Here, hoe, and lose my fucking number."

"Fuck you, hoe ass nigga," I heard as I slammed the door behind me. I started to head back in and teach the young hoe some manners but I had bigger problems.

***

As I cruised down Loop 12, going towards the Grove, I let that bullshit meeting I had called, cross my mind.

Right before I got that video of my wife being a hoe, we had just discussed how the Crew followed her lead as opposed to mine. We had also come up with a solution that I had, as of then, never got to put into play.

Nope, instead I fell back into typical Money shenanigans. Pussy. I definitely saw at that meeting though, that shit wasn't going to work out well for me. I let my mind flash back to the meeting. I realized I was going to have to do one of two things: make up with my wife and the Queens, or go to war with them.

***

"Bobby, I need you to call everyone and get them to meet me at the warehouse in Mesquite, cuz." I said it like I believed in my heart that everyone would still follow me. I chose to ignore the love and respect I knew everyone carried for Schina. I tried to become the boss ass nigga I needed to be.

I knew some of them had to feel some kind of way about following behind a woman, and now that Blue wasn't around, I chose to play on that.

"Let them know I said it's time for the men to take over. I've let Schina flex for too muhfucking long, bruh."

I was greeted by a long silence, followed by a sigh. I could only hold my breath as I waited for his reply. If Bobby had flipped to Schina and them's side, I might as well carry my ass back to Cleveland. He had been the main one in my ear, talking 'bout how was I gone let my bitch wear my boxers.

"It's about time, my nigga. You know me and mine gone roll with you," he said calmly, almost too calmly for my likes. "But you know you late, bruh. Most them pussy ass niggas gone roll wit Schina n'em. And now that she laid up, my nigga, I'd wear my vest. All the time, too, cuz."

"You let me worry about Schina. She ain't gone do shit to me, or step on my toes. At the end of the day, that's still and will always be my bitch. You just worry about getting as many niggas rounded up as possible. Even if you have to step outside of the crew," I demanded with more assurance than I really felt.

I hung up the phone realizing I didn't even have a connect. Schina and her hot head ass had killed Snake. I was sure Jorge wasn't going to fuck with me.

An idea popped into my head and I made a quick phone call.

***

I walked into the warehouse that was sitting off of Highway 80 in Mesquite, a quiet suburb that cornered up to Pleasant Grove. The location made it accessible to hood niggas from all over. I was hoping to see plenty of them at the meeting. But I knew not to wish too hard.

"Here this nigga go," I heard to my left, causing me to tighten my grip on the matte black .9mm I carried. I mentally tightened the straps on the Kevlar I had indeed decided to wear. I had strapped it on under the black t-shirt I was rocking over black jeans. My all-black attire was finished with a pair of all black Air Force One's and an all-black Cleveland Indians base-ball cap.

I let my eyes scan the area to my immediate left noticing it was a young nigga. I had seen him around the hood before, but I ain't know his name. He was a tall lanky dude with braids hanging past his shoulders. He was banging all red and that's what made me open my eyes. That's what made me realize what the meeting was going to look like.

Of course, because of her roots, there would be more niggas whose affiliation was with the bloods that chose to jump ship.

I gave the nigga a head nod as I walked to the middle of the floor. I scanned the warehouse. I couldn't do anything but blame myself for the few amount of people that showed. There was only about thirty, maybe thirty-five, people.

To my surprise, one of 'em was a broad. She was bad as fuck, too. Skin the color of honey, long reddish brown hair that was pulled back in two long corn rolls. Long legs, with thick thighs, that were covered with tight white leggings that clearly showed off her fat ass monkey print. She had a flat stomach, with a belly piercing. Both were on display under the hot pink halter top she wore. The halter matched the hot pink and white Adidas she was pacing the floor in.

I shook my head and tried to focus as I took inventory of who else had shown and who hadn't.

***

Paloma was her name. Her friends called her Bam. To that very day, I didn't know why. Didn't really care to know either.

All that mattered was that bitch knew how to bust her guns. She fucked like a porn star and sucked dick like a white girl. I had been staying with her since the night of the meeting. I knew I was wrong for letting her think there was a chance of us ever having a real relationship, but right then it was convenient. As I pulled into her driveway, I lit a Newport and sat in silence. I hated that I had picked up the habit, but shit was stupid in the streets. I sat there for thirty minutes before I saw the curtains flutter, one too many times. I knew if I didn't go in, she would come out.

Chapter Three
Blue

"Brown, pack it up. Someone sprung for you." I thought I was dreaming until I looked up and saw my cellie staring at me. When it hit me that it was a reality, I quickly hopped off my bunk. All I grabbed was my paperwork. I didn't give a damn 'bout nothing in that pissy ass cell. I didn't even care about that boot leg ass phone. Let 'em find it.

"Damn, bruh, thought you said you was sitting 'til trial, my nigga." He was speaking my thoughts out loud. For some reason it pissed me off, though.

"I'm a grown ass man, dawg," I replied with unneeded attitude. Dude had been cool since they moved me to that pod.

"Damn dawg, I 'ont know what ya problem is, but it ain't got shit to do wit with ya boy. Yo, miss me with the extras," dude said raising up off his bunk.

I wasn't even worried about it as I shrugged his words off. I just headed out the cell and in the direction of my freedom. The whole way through discharge the lil homies words played in my head. I had thought I would be sitting until I went to trial, too. Knowing someone had bailed me out left me with too many unanswered questions. I liked knowing what was going on at all times.

While, hell yea, I wanted to hit the streets before I started my time, I also didn't wanna be caught up in no more of Money's shit. Yea, that was my brother from another mother, but I had grown tired of him taking my ass down with him.

And I knew no-one would go against Schina's wishes. No-one but that fool, anyway. And we all knew the only reason he was willing to do it then was because he had himself stuck out.

As I walked out into the blazing sun, I saw Brionna standing against a bad ass Mercedes SUV. There was a sharp contrast between the sunshine yellow Maxi dress she wore and the all black exterior of the luxury truck gleaming behind her. The truck sat on 22" Forgiato Basamento's. I had to admit that truck was looking too right.

"Hey, Blue. Come on, you've got places to be, brother." Bri said before skipping off to the driver's seat. I continued my leisurely stroll to the truck. I was in no hurry to get anywhere. I definitely wasn't in a hurry to talk to anyone. I just wanted to enjoy the feel of the air in the free world. Fucking with Money's ass there was no telling how long I'd get to enjoy it. I knew if this was all Money's decision, Schina would have my ass back behind the wall before I could even bust a nut.

I climbed in the truck and I was even more impressed. It was also the inside that let me know who had bought the truck. The interior was all black as well. It was the pink engravings that spilled the beans, though. The front seats had hot pink engravings that said Bri. The B's in both seats had crowns etched onto them. The seats in the back said Fat Mack, which is what we all called Bri's daughter, Makayla. The F's in her name wore tiaras. The truck definitely came from her sister-in-law.

"Buckle up, bruh," she said as she blasted Lil' Boosie.

***

As we pulled up to my house, a four bedroom ranch style home in Garland, Bri pulled out a brand new iPhone 6. I never knew how she could find anything in her purse. Every purse I'd ever seen her carry was damn near suitcase size. But she would always stick her hand in and come right out with whatever she was searching for.

"Here Bro," she said as she handed me the phone. "Everyone and anyone who needs the number to this phone already has it. Get another phone for your extra shit."

I looked at her with a mixture of confusion and amusement. When did Bri have anything to do with what we had going on? And who all had the number to this phone? I started to run at least those two questions by her, when I heard another phone ringing.

I watched Bri pull another iPhone from her purse. This one was the same shade of yellow as her dress. There was no doubt she had cases to match every outfit she owned. Money and Schina had her spoiled. The only good thing was, she was still down-to-earth. As a matter of fact, that was as bossy as I had ever heard her be. If shit wasn't already crazy as hell, I might have felt some kind of way about that. That version of Bri screamed Schina. But I really didn't know who was loyal to who.

"Yep, I'm dropping him at his house now." I wondered who she was talking to. I wanted to ask but she kept on with her conversation like I wasn't even sitting there. "Yes, I gave him the phone. It's all up to you, him, and them at this point. I'm dumping his ass and going home to Kayla. We have a date to watch the new Paw Patrol movie."

As she finished her sentence, she looked me in my eye. She got quiet for a second before she said, "You heard me, Blue. I did my part. Now I suggest you do yours. Now get out of my truck. You fucking stink. Got it smelling like penitentiary up in here. Get out."

I just shook my head, grabbed my paperwork and the cell phone, and hopped my ass out of her truck. I would worry about her attitude change at another time. Right then, I just wanted a shower, a blunt, and a nap.

As I walked up the steps to unlock my front door, I heard a weird jingling noise. Just as I started patting for a pistol that wasn't there, I realized it was the phone. Damn, I couldn't even get in the house before the shit started.

The screen lit up informing me I had an awaiting text message. Well that was one message that was going to have to wait. I *did* stink and I needed a damn shower.

After relaxing under the shower heads for at least forty five minutes, I finally drug myself out. I decided to let my body air-dry. Just as I was about to stretch out across my bed, I heard my new phone make that jingle noise again. I strolled over to the dresser and quickly snatched it up.

I need you at the warehouse in Mesquite by 8pm. The name saved for the contact was, That Nigga. I could only assume it was Money. At that moment though, I couldn't help but to wonder if he really was *that* nigga.

I shrugged my shoulders as I noticed it was already six o'clock. I needed to get a move on. I was starving so I was going to need to stop and get something on the way.

It seemed like as soon as I had dressed and decided to take the Ducati Super Sport, my phone rang. I had just purchased the bike a week before I had got knocked. I thought about not answering the call so I could admire my baby a little longer, but I vetoed that idea.

I looked at the screen and it read *A True Boss*. Oh they were already on my nerves with the bullshit, and again, the idea of branching out on my own crossed my mind.

"Hello," I said, wondering who's voice I was about to hear.

"You've got a meeting at 8. Make that meeting and play nice. Before you go, you should know *we* are the ones who decided to bring you home. Let your boy keep pretending he is the one. But all you have to do is look at your bond papers. They won't lie. After your meeting, your presence is expected. I will text you the location once you have left there. Choose your loyalties wisely Tyrone."

I'd know that voice anywhere. Nicole. Of course the Queens would choose her to contact me. We had been fucking for months. I guess Ivory and Schina didn't realize that's all it was between us. Sex. Yea, I fed her info about Money. At the time, I was trying to come between Schina and Money. I needed my homie to man the fuck up. Now, I was just interested in seeing what the fuck was going on.

Of course I knew about the girls missing. And I knew that some shit had went down between Schina and Money. I knew Money had left Schina in a coma. But that's about all I knew.

Knowing I needed to get a move on, I scanned my bond papers and sure enough it said Queens Inc. I grabbed my keys and headed to the garage with my mind shooting into overdrive.

***

I pulled up to the warehouse with five minutes to spare. I saw Money's old Tahoe and I figured he had gotten it back from June Bug's mom for one reason or another.

I texted Money and let him know I was going to smoke a square before I came in. As I lit my Kool, I glanced around the parking lot. There were maybe ten cars spread around. Of course, I realized most of the crew had probably decided to rock with the girls. I also knew I had to make a decision on what I was going to do as well. Right then, I was just going to go with the flow.

Chapter Four
Schina

I had been awake for and a week and I still hadn't quite grasped what the fuck was going on. I got that my kids were missing. I got that Money's ass had been AWOL. I even got that Money called himself trying to take over the crew. What I wasn't fucking grasping was why more wasn't being fucking done.

"Man, get the fucking doctor in here now!" I knew that I had to look like a psycho, but I didn't even care. I had to get the hell out of the hospital. I needed to go find my children. Obviously, it wasn't going to be as serious to anyone else as it was to me. That meant I needed off my ass and on my mother fucking feet. ASAP.

"Mrs. Morgan, we have called Dr. Esedebe and he is on his way." Hearing her say Dr. Esedebe threw me for a loop. It also managed to take my attitude from a ten to a hundred.

"Bitch, I said call my gen-e-ral prac-tit-ion-er." I pronounced it for her like she was hard of hearing, or slow. She had to be one or the other. "What fucking use is an obstetrician going to do me?" I saw Ivory exchange looks with the nurse. It was then I realized what the hell was going on. "Oh hell fuck no! No way. Ivory please tell me y'all are bullshitting. I can't be..."

"Pregnant. Actually, Schina, yes, you are," a deep voice with a heavy Africa accent responded. I knew without turning it was my ob/gyn. I had been using the same doctor since I got pregnant with Tai, so I would recognize his voice anywhere.

Tears sprang to my eyes and I had the sudden urge to kill someone. The only problem was, there wasn't anyone on my immediate list. Well, except my bum ass husband, Byron. And even he got a pass, at least until I found my babies. "Ivory. Get. Me. Out. Of. Here."

Ivory gave the nurse an apologetic look before she brought over a set of clothes she had picked up for me. I snatched the clothes and headed to the attached bathroom. "Great fucking job, Schina. You go and get pregnant by that hoe ass nigga. Again."

I was so disappointed in myself. I not only fell for his lies, I failed to protect myself. Fuck, what if he gave me something? I snatched the door open. I was hoping Dr. Esedebe was still in the room. Once I saw his face, I rushed back in his direction. "Please, Doctor, tell me he didn't give me anything. Please tell me I'm not going to have to go for that nigga's head." I was so pissed, I didn't even care about having said too much.

The doctor put a reassuring arm around my shoulders before he spoke. "No, Schina. Your STD screening was clean. Besides being four weeks pregnant, you're fine. I know what's going on with your daughters, so I won't tell you don't stress. But I will say, you need to try to take it as easy as possible. I'm sure you already know, but we will be considering this a high-risk pregnancy. I've written you a prescription for a high dosage prenatal vitamin. And no matter what, I want to see you in my office in two weeks. Call Marjorie and make the appointment first thing in the morning. You also need to go in to see your general practitioner soon. Schina, you need to be at full capacity to find your girls. Please, take care of yourself."

I nodded as I headed back into the bathroom. Tears of relief were prickling the back of my eyelids. *At least something is right in the world*, I thought as my hand shot instinctively to my still flat stomach. *I can't believe this shit*, I thought as I slammed the bathroom door in anger.

***

"Ivory, what the hell am I gonna do? Where the hell is Nicole? Where are my kids? Who has them? Has there been any word on my husband?" I shot my words at my best friend in machine gun fashion. I stared at the side of her head as we rode. We were safely seated in the middle seat of an all-black Suburban. It was being driven by none other than that nigga Blue. Beside him, of course, sat Funky Town. That was my boy, and he would forever have my back. Behind us were two pure bred midnight black German Shepherds, Delgado and Chloe. I had named them after two dogs from the movie Beverly Hills Chihuahua. I loved that movie.

"Bitch, I don't know what you're gonna do. Other than have that baby, anyway. I mean, that's all you can do. I don't know who has the girls or where they are. The kidnappers left the one note and we haven't heard from them since. I have a feeling they've been waiting for you. Money ass is laid up wit some bitch from the south named Paloma. I let that nigga make it cuz you know how you get." She responded, but I noticed she left out her answer about Nicole.

"Where the hell is Nicole? I swear I ain't seen her but maybe three or four times. What's up with that? Please tell me you ain't beat that girl up again." I laughed until I noticed Ivory never changed the scowl that marred her beautiful face. "Bitch, speak."

"You don't want these problems, hoe," Ivory said jokingly before she quickly got serious again. "I don't know what's up wit ya girl. She been real funny acting. I just been keeping her at arm's length. *But,* I *will* say, she been on top of the traps. The money coming in and the dope going out. Everything's adding up right. Hell, sometimes we end up with too much money. So I thought fuck it. She don't bother me, I don't bother her."

There was so much to take in. But first thing first, I needed my phone. Someone had to know something about my girls. I turned to Ivory and before I could say a word, she was tapping on Funky Town's shoulder. "Hand me that phone out the glove box, bruh." I watched as he reached his baseball mitt sized hands in the glove box. I also watched as he pulled out a hot pink LG G4. "We have someone tracking all incoming text messages and phone calls to *that* phone, so keep it on you. Everything from your old phone is synced, so work some magic."

She was right. I usually always had someone to call to get shit done, but I didn't know what I needed done. I decided to start with my so-called circle. I scrolled down to the H's. Normally Money was stored there under husband. I didn't see husband but I laughed deeply when I saw his picture. Someone had saved him under Hoe Ass Nigga. I glanced at Ivory who was peering out the window, attempting to look innocent. I just continued to laugh as I pressed send.

"I'm sorry the number you are attempting to reach has been disconnected."

"Ain't this a bitch," I said out loud. Without another word, I scrolled a little further down until I got to Jorge's number.

After a couple of rings, I heard a heavy Mexican accent say, "Hola, mija. I'm glad you're up and moving around. What can I do to help mija?" Jorge had taken a liking to me immediately. That was one of the biggest issues between Money and I right before I thought we made up.

"Hello, Jorge," I responded. "It's good to be up and moving around, too. I need two favors. Please just ask around 'bout my daughters, anyone with any information will be paid accordingly. And two, can you call Blacc and see if he has Byron's phone number?"

"I already have all of my ears open for any news on the girls. I have even offered my own reward. I will have that number for you within ten minutes." *Click.* Jorge disconnected without another word.

I decided to call the missing link of our triumvirate while I waited for him to get me the number. As I listened to her phone ring, I laid my head against the headrest. I took a moment to close my eyes. The doctor had warned me I was likely to have headaches and damn was he right. Not only had I had trauma, I was sure I needed to feed the baby. Just as I started to dwell on that, I heard Nicole answer the phone.

"What," her voice was breathy and almost impatient.

"Bitch, what you mean what? You think you'd be excited to hear from me. Or explaining how come you are not assisting in the search for my children. But I guess I'm tripping." I knew my voice was filled with just as much attitude.

"Oh, hey Schina," she shot back. Her voice damn sure didn't lose the hint of impatience, though. "I'm just out making shit happen. I'm making sure everyone had their ears open, but the street shit still has to continue. Remember, we have a quota to meet now."

I didn't like her attitude, but she did have a point. I could just hope she ain't start feeling herself. I was and would always be, the H.B.I.C. "I hear you. But you make sure you don't forget, there can only be one boss. That's still me," I reminded her as I heard a beep, letting me know I had a text coming through. "Anyway, I'ma holla at you later."

I pulled the phone away from my ear and pressed end call. I immediately switched into my messages screen. Just as I thought, I had received a text from Jorge. It had a phone number and a message that said, "Little one, I know you didn't ask this of me, but I knew eventually you would come for the information. Byron has been getting his needs met by my son, Blacc, as you all call him. I have let him carry on, just so I can keep tabs on the both of them. Tell me when you are ready for me to cut them both off."

I smiled inside as I tapped the number he had sent. As the phone rang, I started digging in Ivory's purse. I knew she had a blunt in there. I could definitely use one. "Blue, stop at Whataburger before we get to the house. I'ma need to eat. And Ivory, damn, I know you got some weed in this big ass purse."

"Yea," a female's voice finally answered. I had to glance at the phone and make sure I hadn't disconnected and dialed someone else.

"May I speak to Byron?" I figured I'd play this the respectful way, unless ole girl decided to make this a death scene. Hopefully she knew who I was and would stay in her own damn lane.

"Who the fuck is this? You know what, I don't even give a fuck. Get off my nigga's line." *Click.*

Death scene, I thought, just as I noticed we were pulling into the Whataburger closest to my house. "Order enough for Delgado and Chloe begging asses too," I ordered as I laid my pounding head back against the headrest.

***

As we pulled up to my house in pretty Rowlett, the sun had just descended enough to let the shadows of my two trees touch. It would be completely dark in about thirty minutes, so I knew it had to be about 8:30. Even though it was night and September, it was still hot as hell outside. So hot as soon as I stepped from the truck, I broke a sweat. I just grabbed my food. I knew Funky Town would grab my dogs and Ivory would grab all of the things that I had brought home from the hospital. And that included what looked like fifty damn prescriptions.

I kind of drug my body onto my porch and reluctantly stuck my key in the lock. The last time I had been there, my family was intact. Money and I were on our way to the meeting with Jorge, and the girls were getting ready to enjoy a day with their nanny, Ms. Thomas.

I swung the door open, and just like I knew would happen, I was slammed with images of happier times. The banner the girls had made for Money's homecoming was still strung across the living room. The dead balloons were laying in piles all over the room. I was hit with a wave of nausea and I made a beeline for the guest bathroom. I barely had time to lift the lid before I released nothing but bile into the toilet. I felt someone lifting my hair from my shoulders, and placing it into a ponytail. I immediately knew it was Ivory. Damn, I needed to do something special for her. As soon as we found my girls, I would find a way to thank her for all that she did for me.

"Thanks, Bestie. I'm going to bed. Please have one of them niggas get that shit outta my living room. In the morning, we are going to pay my husband a visit so get this Petunia's..."

"Paloma, bitch. Her name is Paloma."

"I wouldn't give a fuck if her name was Donald Fucking Trump. Get her address." I knew I was yelling at the wrong person. I didn't care. I was hot, tired, and I needed my daughters home.

Chapter Five
Money

"Bam, if I order some food from IHOP, you gone go pick it up?" I asked her the question already knowing how she was going to act.

"Why I gotta go pick it up, Byron," she asked as she stuck her head out of the cluttered closet. She called herself in there cleaning up. The only problem with that was her idea of cleaning up wasn't what my wife had me accustomed to. She would shuffle shit around, bag up trash, and do dishes, but that was about it. I hated that I had gotten myself into this predicament. Then I had to add in the fact that the broad had to question everything I said. I was really starting to realize how good I had it. I also had to realize, chances were, I had fucked it all up.

"Because I'm your man and I asked you to." I wouldn't have had to go through all the extra shit if I was at home with my wife. Hell, I wouldn't have even been ordering food. At home, as soon as I opened my eyes, shawty would have been cooking for a nigga.

When I looked up and saw old girl still staring at me, I finally snapped. "Why the hell are you standing there looking stupid? You know what, fuck it. I'll go pick up the food my damn self." I swung my legs off the bed and headed to the closet. I grabbed one of the few outfits I had there. I hadn't done much shopping and I didn't grab anything from the house. I wasn't moving a damn thing out of the house I shared with my wife. There were two reasons for that decision. One, in my head, I didn't think I had accepted that it was truly over. Shawty lived by loyalty, and I was banking on that. The second and probably most important reason, I wasn't sure one of her crazy ass Queens didn't have a sniper sitting outside the house. For all I knew, they were just waiting on my black ass to show up.

"Damn, Byron. What you gone do is stop talking to me like that," Bam started whining, but I wasn't hearing that shit. I just kept on getting dressed. As I was throwing on a pair of black basketball shorts, she continued with her complaints. "I bet you ain't talk to that whore like that. So you ain't gonna..."

I grabbed my keys and was out of the room before she could even finish her sentence. Hell, until I received that video, I had never had a reason to talk to Schina like that. And when I looked back on it, I still didn't have a reason to.

Logically speaking, I had been locked up for putting my hands on a bitch I had been creeping with. A chic my wife ended up having to kill, because she gave my dope away to a nigga she knew I hated.

"Man, I really fucked up," I scolded myself as I climbed into the old Tahoe. I couldn't believe I had given up my old lifestyle behind some bullshit. As I turned on the truck and waited for the air to cool off the interior, I slid in my Jay-Z Blueprint album. I skipped to *Song Cry*. As the beginning instrumentals hit, I reached in the glove box and pulled out a bag of some shit called cookies n cream kush. I hadn't had a chance to sample it yet. On the way to get food seemed to be as good a time as any.

***

After I picked up the food, I stopped at the corner store. I needed to get some cigars and snacks for later. It was Sunday and the beginning of football season, so I planned on spending most of the day at home watching television. I figured I would order pizza and wings for dinner. Lord knew Bam wasn't cooking shit.

Once I pulled up to the block I was residing at, I happened to notice not one, but two black Suburbans parked on the street. I started to turn around and go somewhere else, but I figured I was tripping. Schina hadn't been awake long enough to already be popping up at a nigga's house. At least that's what I was hoping, anyway.

I parked the truck and opened the door as I reached across to grab the food. I turned to the back, trying to grab the bags from the corner store. Just as I got a handle on everything, I heard it. *Click, clack.* The sound of a gun being taken off safety and a bullet being chambered. "Fuck." I had damn sure gotten caught slipping.

"That's ya problem. That's all you think about. Fucking." As soon as I recognized Ivory's voice, I wanted to scan the area for my wife. But I knew better than making any moves. "Yea, she's here, too. She's in there with ya new little plaything. Grab ya shit and walk very slowly, nigga. Walk your disloyal ass right into your new house. Don't try anything stupid. I'm sure you know I'm not the only one out here. Even though I doubt anyone wants ya hoe ass dead more than I do."

I knew she was serious so I just grabbed the bags and eased the rest of the way out of the truck. I used my foot to shut the door and headed to the porch. I knew Schina very well, so I knew better than to even bother speculating on what I was about to walk into. As I reached the front door, I saw Ivory's hand reach around me to turn the knob. For a moment, I thought about dropping the food and trying to make a run for it. That's when I heard a male voice.

"Nah, playa. Just walk yo ass up in there. Go on and take your punishment like the man you're supposed to be." I wasn't sure, but it sounded a lot like Funky Town. I knew if it was him, shit was about to get real ugly. I knew I should have moved my ass into one of those nosy ass neighborhoods, but it was too late for regrets.

As the door swung open, I saw Schina sitting on the coffee table. Her outfit let me know she was there to play no games, not with Bam or me. She had on a black wife beater paired with some black leggings. On her feet, she had on a nondescript pair of black tennis shoes, and she rocked an all-black Pittsburgh Steelers cap. I could see the bandages on her arm where the IV's had been removed, and I had a moment of remorse.

"Hello, Byron," her voice still sounded like singing angels to me. I knew though, the only angel that had anything to do with this situation was Lucifer. "Before you say anything slick, I'd take a look around the room. Check out the company I brought with me and definitely get a look at ya lil girlfriend's face."

I had been so mesmerized by the fact that my wife was sitting so casually in my newest place of residence, I hadn't even noticed there were others in the room. Before I could take stock of what I was facing, I was shoved further into the room.

"Go on closer so you can get the full visual, nigga." Yea, it was definitely Funky Town. I decided to just do what they demanded. I could only hope that somehow I could use the girls- no, better not try that- I'd try to use Schina's love for me to at least save my own ass.

I dropped the bags on a table beside the door and walked further into the room. I took that moment to do a full scan of the room. Knowing who all was there would help me determine if I was walking away or not. I noticed Chris in one corner holding an MP-5. I noticed Chance standing at the entrance to the hall. He looked like he had two Desert Eagles. Skeet was standing in the entrance to the kitchen, this nigga had two MP-5s. I knew Funky Town was behind me, him and Ivory. I didn't know what kind of guns they carried, but I knew it was safe to say they had something big and heavy too.

"Where's Bam," I asked. No one answered, but as I drew near to the couch, I saw her anyway. She was still alive, but I only knew that by the pain that shone brightly in her eyes. After watching for a few seconds, I saw the slight rise and fall of her chest. Her nose, which used to be small and adorable, was swollen twice its normal size. There was a gash the size of my index finger across her forehead. Her lips that used to look so sexy sliding up and down my dick, looked like hot links. I couldn't do anything but shake my head. I could only hope that we made it out of the situation alive. Well, at least me. While I liked Paloma, only bitch I ever loved was the monster who had done this to her.

"Damn, Schina, you ain't have to do her like that." Before she even opened her mouth, I knew I had fucked up.

"Nigga, do you remember what happened the last time you had the nerve to ask me about one of your little tricks?"

Hell yea, I remembered. First, she showed up to visitation looking like a damn cripette. She then proceeded to give me a step by step rundown on how she tortured and burned that bitch, Bianca. And then, to add insult to injury, she left my ass sitting in jail for two weeks. She claimed she felt like I needed it.

"You're right, Schina."

"But, I'ma give you the courtesy of knowing exactly what got this hoe's ass whooped. I don't want you to be under the impression this had a damn thing to do with you. Cuz it didn't. Nah, when I called your phone last night..."

"Wait, you called my phone? I don't have any missed calls from you."

"I know you don't. As I was saying, when I called your phone last night, this thot answered. Now I tried to be respectful, seeing as to how I was calling *her* man and all," even the deaf man down the block could hear the sarcasm in her voice. "So I was nice. I used my white girl voice and everything. But this dumb bitch, I guess she didn't get the memo. I guess no one called and let her know mama is awake. Instead of finding out who I was, she immediately starting going left. Bitch told me fuck me. *Me!*" She punctuated her anger by slamming her palm onto the wooded table top. She had Paloma so shook, when her palm connected, she visibly lurched.

"Shawty, but how you just gone…" Of course she didn't let me finish my sentence before she started back up. But it wasn't even her words that made my back go rigid. It was the fact that she was reaching in her waist band. She pulled out two guns I hadn't seen before. I figured those were the .50 calibers she had told me about when we were in Mexico. I guessed she had finally gotten around to naming them. Shit. That couldn't be a good thing.

"First off, nigga, you should know you have given up all rights to call me that fuck ass name. Second, you should also know there ain't a bitch in my city that can get away with disrespecting the Queen of this muhfucka."

I couldn't do anything but lower my head. I knew if I tried to help Bam out anymore, I was only going to be the cause of her death. Regardless of how bad I fucked up, I knew my wife. To hear me coming to another woman's defense was just going to further enrage her.

"Nigga, go have a seat next to ya plaything," I heard Ivory demand. To emphasize her point, she nudged me in my back with her gun. I was pretty certain I felt a silencer. That meant she was still carrying her P9s. Shit, us surviving the visit was looking less and less likely. I wondered if there was anything I could say or do to balance the odds. I seriously doubted it. I pondered it, though, as I indeed headed over to the couch. I watched as Bam writhed in pain. I wanted to feel bad for her, but I needed to figure out how to save my life.

"Now Money," Schina spoke with an unexpected tone of patience. "When I first called your phone last night, I only wanted to let you know a couple of things. But like I said, Paloma here, decided to get disrespectful. So now I'm here, and I may as well deliver my message in person. Well, my messages. First, you are released from your duties as a father. Since you can't seem to find time to look for *our* missing daughters, you no longer have to worry about them at all. Second, you are released from your position in the crew. You no longer have a spot with those who have rode for you forever my nigga." I started to respond but she threw her hand up and continued on like I wasn't shit. "Now, I know where you've been getting your dope from. I have decided that in honor of what we once had, to let you hold on to that for two weeks, or until I find my daughters, whichever comes first. After that, you are done in Dallas. You can pack up Miss Molly over there and take your ass on back to the Land. Dallas is no longer your home, bitch nigga."

I tried to process everything she had just said. I was having a hard time getting past the part where she said I no longer had any children. I mean, nah, I hadn't been looking as hard as she was about to do, but hell, who had the connections Schina had? But I was smart enough to know to just go along with what she was saying, at least for the moment. "I hear you Schina."

"I know you hear me, husband." Her voice was dripping with sarcasm. I'm sure I also heard a deeper tone of anger and hurt. "I just hope your simple ass is listening to what the fuck I'm saying, bruh. Two weeks at *max*, Money. Don't test my gangsta. Let's go y'all."

As I watched everyone file out of my house, I noticed that one of the Suburbans had pulled directly in front of the house. I couldn't help but to wonder who was driving.

"Bye, bitches," Ivory taunted as she slammed the door behind her. She seemed to have gotten some satisfaction out of the confrontation. I could only imagine how much she wanted to off my ass, though.

I waited a few minutes until I felt like it was safe before I got up to lock the door. On the way back to the couch, I realized I hadn't heard Bam moaning. She wasn't making any of the hurt noises I had heard when I first got back. "Fuck, don't let her ass be dead," I muttered to myself as I mentally began counting up the bodies that had dropped behind my infidelities. I had a strong feeling that list wasn't through growing.

Chapter Six
S

I hated Schina and Money both. They had both caused me immeasurable pain and taken people and things away from me that I would never be able to replace. Therefore, I would also never be able to forgive them. That's why I took their bad ass kids. Nah, even under the circumstances, Thing One and Two, as I had taken to calling them, were very well mannered, besides the youngest one doing a lot of damn crying, and eating. I had been thinking about sending their asses back home off the simple fact I couldn't afford to feed her little fat ass.

"Miss Ma'am," Thing One said. She looked just like her mama, making it easy to not like her. I did, however, notice that her outfit was getting dingy. I knew I needed to bathe them. I had been trying to take decent care of them, but hell I ain't have no kids. How the hell was I supposed to know what to do?

"What, child," I asked impatiently. I had been preparing myself to contact Schina for the first time when she interrupted my thoughts.

"We are hungry. And bored." Her face was sullen and I watched her place her hands where her hips one day would be. She didn't stop there, though. "You said you were just keeping us safe until my mama or daddy showed up. If you really knew our parents, you would know what we like. And we wouldn't be staying in a place like this. None of mama's friends live in places like this. And everyone mama lets us hang out with, has cool stuff, just so we are never bored. My mama makes sure of it."

Hearing her say all that seemed to get her little sister going, too. "Yea, all of mama's friend's houses have lots of rooms. And you only have a couple. Plus, mama always gives her friends money to take us places. Why we can't go nowhere?"

Oh your mama is going to give me money to take y'all places, I thought, as I took a subconscious look around my apartment. I lived in an efficiency in an apartment complex off of Munger in the East Dallas side of town. My whole apartment was virtually one room, aside from the bathroom. I had never had an issue with it. It had definitely come in handy once I had received the children. They could never get out of my sight if there was nowhere for them to go.

But when those spoiled ass children pointed it out, I couldn't help but to be depressed by my surroundings. It was all good, though. I was going to get everything that was owed to me and then some.

"Go look in the fridge," I said distractedly. I was thinking of how my life used to be. When my whole family was intact, I was spoiled, too. My parents weren't shit, but as the only sister, once my brothers started running the streets, I was well taken care of. Anything my heart desired was delivered to my fine ass on a platter. Yea, I used to be fine, too. Five feet two inches, one hundred thirty pounds of pure sexy. Brown eyes like a Hershey candy bar. I kept a short pixie cut with honey blond streaks. And my skin... I had the prettiest black skin, no acne and I never needed makeup. I was no longer any of that, though.

"There's just junk in there Ms. Ma'am," the voice of Thing Two pulled me from my reminiscing. "Can you cook us some real food? I want some fried chicken."

"I want some pork chops," Thing one decided to put in her order, too. What the fuck they thought this was... Burger King?

"I'm not cooking shit, but if y'all will sit down and shut the hell up, watch some TV or something, I'll order some pizza and pasta. Y'all seem to like that."

Both girls sighed, and headed to the TV. I figured I was going to have to start cooking if I wanted to keep them happy and quiet.

I would need some food for that to happen, though. I knew just who to call.

I made the call to the pizza place and to my partner in crime. At least this crime, anyway. I told her to bring 'real food' and I also ordered them some tablets equipped with 4g. I really couldn't afford it on my already dwindling account, but I knew it would get greater later.

***

"Thanks Ms. Ma'am," the girls cried in unison as I called them over to hand them their pizza.

I almost felt bad, they were behaving so well. But fuck their family. Just as their parents fucked over mine. On three separate occasions.

Just as they sat back down in front of the TV, I heard a rhythmic knocking on the door. I knew who it was, so I quickly walked over and opened the door. I was more than thankful for the interruption. I was sure I had seen the airing episode of *Jessie* fifty times.

"Damn, that was quick," I said as my guest walked in with their hands full of Walmart bags. "I didn't expect you to get here so soon."

"I had to come while my dude was gone. I know he ain't gonna be gone long, so I have to go." She quickly dropped the bags, except one. She handed me that one carefully. I noticed she wouldn't look me in my face. I started to ask her about it, but I knew that would come with drama. Drama I simply didn't have time for.

"These are the tablets. You'll have to activate them but they are on a Metro plan so they have the 4g you requested, even though I don't know why you are catering to the little fucks. Remember why we even took them, bitch. Don't get it twisted."

"Damn, babe. I know what we are doing and why. I also know in order to keep them quiet, I have to keep them happy.

Hell, they've been here for three damn weeks with nothing but the Disney Channel." I saw the doubt cross her face and so I tried to turn her face so I could kiss her lips. She flinched and pulled away from me as she started heading to the door. "What the fuck is up with that?" She had never turned down my kisses and I was pissed.

"Nothing. I gotta go. I'ma text you later because we need to wrap this shit up. I'm tired of living this charade."

I finally got a peek of her face. I couldn't see much with the way her hat sat so low, but I saw enough. I wanted to ask her about it, but she was gone before I could find the words. Oh well, she would tell me about it when she was ready. I had to get back to the kids.

After I got the groceries put away and the girls settled with their tablets, it was time for me to send message number one. Schina was going to lose her mind.

***

"Girls," I called.

Yes, Ms. Ma'am," Thing One turned to me first. When she saw the tablets in my hand, her eyes lit up. She jumped to her feet faster than I would have thought was possible. Not even knowing what was going on, her sister quickly jumped up beside her. The loyalty between those two was incredible.

"Ooooh, are those for us," the younger one asked excitedly after finally seeing what her sister had seen. When I nodded my head yes, both girls hurriedly rushed in my direction.

Just as they reached for them, I snatched them out of their reach. The disappointment on their faces was instant. I almost started to feel bad. I had to be careful. I could feel myself bonding with them. That definitely wasn't a part of the plan.

"Just listen to me for a minute and y'all can have them, okay?" I waited for both heads to nod in agreement before I continued. "No texting apps and no social media. I have these linked to my phone and if you try to contact your parents I will know. Do y'all understand?" I fully expected them to question why they couldn't talk to their parents, but they didn't. They both just nodded in agreement. Once I was sure they believed my lie, I handed over the tablets. As I watched them happily trod off to the living room to do whatever it was that kids did on tablets, I began looking around for the burner phone. I had purchased it the very day the girls and I got back to Dallas.

I opened the contacts and stared at the one number I had stored. Schina. I let my mind wander back to the day I got the call that my brother was killed. But before I let it overtake me, I snapped out of it.

"I bet you miss your kids just like I miss my life. I bet you're wondering what I want. $500,000. I really want your head on a platter. I'll settle for the money. You have 48 hours. And go."

I knew I wasn't asking for much. But that was only the beginning. I'd have her drop off the first set and then text her the next day for another $500,000. I wasn't sure if she had it on hand, but I knew about her new connect. I knew they were bringing in way more money than they used to. I was sure for the safety of her children, she would find a way. And if not, well I figured, she didn't need them that bad. I couldn't have kids anyway. I'd just keep them.

Chapter Seven
Schina

"Call Nicole! Now," I demanded. I had just received a text message from someone claiming to have my daughters. I knew Nicole could track anything. I was just hoping whoever had sent the message hadn't used an app and the phone would be traceable.

"What's wrong, Schina? You've got to calm down." I already knew what she was about to say so I beat her to the punch.

"I know. I know. I need to think about the baby. But whoever has my daughters just texted me. I need to know if she can trace this call. Now!" I saw Ivory's eyes get wide as she reached down to the coffee table to grab her phone. We had just got back from my doctor's appointment, where I had been given a clean bill of health. Well as clean as I was going to get for the next seven and a half months. I had also made some stops to talk to a few people. It was really just to let the streets know I was back.

If I didn't get any answers from Nicole about who may have texted me, I was going to suit up. I would be making some more stops later that evening. But the next stops would be ending in mayhem.

"Nicole, says she was already on the way. She had some ideas she wanted to run by you anyway. But Schina, I don't trust her. I know she's been down with us for a while, but something about her movements lately have been off. I just want you to know I ain't feeling it. I know that's ya girl, but as soon as I have evidence that she's up to some funny shit, it's lights out for her ass." I absolutely loved the way Ivory's loyalty was set up, so I didn't even question it.

Just as I opened my mouth to agree with what she was saying, I heard a key jingling in the knob. Delgado and Chloe heard it as well. They usually stayed at one trap or another because Money didn't like dogs. But because this was no longer his house, my fur babies were now home. And they weren't having any pop up visits. I laughed as the hair on the back of Delgado's neck stood straight up like soldiers at attention.

"Girl, that's probably Nicole ass right there." Even the dogs turned to stare at Ivory as she got up from the couch. "Guess the bitch thought you were gonna keep the same locks. Dumb ass."

To punctuate her statement, whoever was at the door began impatiently ringing the doorbell. I said whoever, but it could only be Nicole. The only people who had copies of the old keys, and weren't aware of the lock changes, were Nicole and Money. And I knew that fool wasn't crazy enough to show up over here. I watched as Delgado stood firm by my side, but Chloe's bossy ass walked right beside Ivory to go open the door.

Chloe gave off a low growl as I heard Ivory open the door for the incessant doorbell ringer. I could hear Chloe's growl growing deeper, so I grabbed Beauty off the table. I carefully aimed it at the hall door that separated the front entryway from the living room. I knew Ivory wasn't going to allow just anyone in my home, but I wasn't taking any chances. Hell, just three weeks ago my own husband had tried to kill me.

"Bitch, put the fucking gun down. Hell, if I was trouble, Delgado," I heard Nicole say.

"That's Chloe. Delgado never growls before attack," I corrected. I don't know why it bothered me so much that she couldn't tell my babies apart, but it did.

"Chloe, Delgado, whoever, it's not like they're going to allow no bullshit to go down anyway."

"Yea, I know. But a bullet causes less mess for me to have to clean up. But, I didn't call you here to talk about my babies," I said, as I reached down to pet Chloe's head, as she returned to her spot by my feet.

"Yea, Ivory told me what's up. Let me see your phone so I can get the number." While normally I wouldn't have hesitated to hand her my phone, something about Ivory's words, and Chloe's reaction to her made me hesitant.

"Nah, you know I have that face recognition set up now. I'll just forward you the message and phone number. Will that work?" I didn't want her to feel some kind of way. I *needed* her to track the phone. I *needed* to know who had sent that message.

"Yea, that should work." I watched her face trying to judge her reaction. I didn't see anything out of the way, so I just unlocked my phone and sent her the necessary information. I listened to her phone jingle as the message was relayed from my LG to hers.

As I watched her fiddle around on her phone doing whatever it was that she was doing, I had a sudden urge to smoke. I knew Ivory was going to bitch, but I didn't even care.

"I'll be back," I told the other Queens as I headed to my room.

"Just bring the whole sack, bitch," was Ivory's response. I swear her ass knew me better than I knew myself. As I headed into my bedroom, I had to pass the many pictures of my family. When I came to the one when Liv had first came home and Money and Tai were staring at us with complete love, I came to a sudden stop. My sudden stop caused Delgado to slam into the back of my legs. I figured Chloe had stayed back to keep an eye on Nicole.

"My bad, boy," I said to Delgado as I reached down and scratched the top of his head. I raised back up and let my fingertips trail the faces of my family. I would slaughter the entire world to have these days back.

I felt a tear trickle down my face as I headed to my bedroom. When I walked in my room, I could still faintly smell Money's John Paul Gautlier cologne. The tears started to run more freely as I realized what had become of my marriage. I couldn't believe that nigga had put his hands on me like that. If I tried to kill his ass for every time he stepped out on our marriage, I'd be on death row. As I thought of all the bullshit he had put me through, my tears dried up. My body was quickly overcome with anger. Fuck that nigga.

I grabbed my sack of weed and a pack of Blazing Fire Swisher Sweets and headed back to the living room. The tension was thick as I went to take my seat back on the couch. I could tell some words had been said between my two best friends, but I would have to handle all of that later.

"Please, Nicole, tell me you found something."

I heard her take a deep breath before answering. "Well it's an unregistered phone, so I can't tell you who it is. All I can tell you is the phone is somewhere in East Dallas."

I could tell they were hurting as bad as I was because the room was silent. You couldn't even hear the usual panting of the dogs. It's like even they could tell shit was about to get ugly.

"Well, they said I had two days to come up with $500,000. That's no big deal with all of the work you have been moving for us, right Nicole?" Even if she came with some bullshit, it wasn't an issue. Jorge had offered a million dollars reward and I was more than willing to take him up on that. I just had to see if she was going to try to play me behind my money. I'd hate to splatter her brains on the walls, but I was not in the mood for any games.

"Girl, we gonna have to sit down and discuss your finances as soon as the girls are home safely. But, to answer your question, nah, that's chump change nowadays. I can go get that bagged up tonight. I do need to go make some runs, if you don't need me." Being satisfied with her answer, I just waved her off. I grabbed a magazine to use to break down some weed.

I thought about my daughters as I continued to break down the weed. I vaguely heard Ivory letting Nicole out as I wondered if my babies were warm. Were they eating? Were they clean?

"Give me the weed before you have it soaking wet," Ivory said as she slid the magazine out of my lap. I watched, still pondering my children's wellbeing, as she rolled two blunts. I noticed one was bigger than the other. I somehow knew the smaller one was for me. I knew it wasn't even worth the fight. I was, after all, six weeks pregnant. The fact that she was even letting me smoke, without a fight, was saying a lot.

I reached over, grabbed my blunt, and lit it as I looked in my best friends eyes. "I need to find my daughters. And I need to show the streets I'm still Shina. Someone is testing my G, Ivory, and I ain't feeling it."

"I'm supposing you want me to call the hot squad?" The Hot Squad is what we called the group of men I called upon when I was about to cause bloodshed. I was definitely about to do that.

I pondered her question as I toked away, thinking of what my move was going to be. "Nah, I don't need all of them. Just call the same ones who rode with us to Money's house," I said as I began coughing. The weed was more potent than I thought.

**

It wasn't quite dark outside but I didn't care. My crew and I rolled up on a house I had spent quite a bit of time in. Unlike usual, where there would be three trucks, that night we were only rolling two trucks deep. And instead of Suburbans, we were in Expeditions.

As usual, Funky Town was my driver, and seated behind him was Money's best friend. Guess Money doesn't make the world go 'round. Behind us was Ivory, Skeet, and Chris. We had left Chance at the junkyard with Delgado and Chloe.

As we parked a few houses down from our designation, I began second-guessing my decision. That was something new to me, but I just chalked it up to nerves. I pushed the doubt to the back of my mind and climbed out of the truck. Blue and Funky climbed out behind me, while Ivory's truck sat running idle.

The neighborhood we were in was too quiet to perform the acts that I had dreamt up. We were just here to collect someone and head to the junkyard. Once I had either coerced the person to come along peacefully, or knocked them the hell out, Ivory's truck would back into the driveway. Funky and Blue would secure them to the custom straps in the storage compartment.

I straightened my all-white outfit and tilted my all-white Rangers cap on my head. I had to make sure my hair and tattoos were all covered.

We decided wearing all black in this heat would be a dead giveaway. Instead, we all wore different colors. Funky was in all green, he said it was because it was Tai's favorite color. Blue was in, of course, all blue.

As I walked up to the door, I had to fight a vicious urge to throw up. I had noticed that this baby had terrible timing. Everything about this pregnancy happened at the wrong damn time. There was nothing I could do about it, so I just sucked it up and continued on with my plans.

I knocked on the door and waited. After two more knocks, finally the door was wrenched open. "Oh, Raschina. What's up? Come on in," my longtime friend Jesus offered.

"Nah, not tonight. I need you to take a ride with me, foo," I half stated, half demanded.

"Okay, let me get my shoes. You wanna come in," he offered again. But I was no damn fool.

"Nah, I'm good," was my simple reply. As I watched him turn to go into the red brick house, I gave the signal for Funky to go around back. I knew Jesus hated dogs so I wasn't worried about that. But I just knew in my heart he was about to make a run for it.

Moments later, just as I thought, I heard the crash of the screen door slapping loudly against the wall. I started heading in that direction, but before I even got there, I heard the whoop of air being knocked out of someone. That was instantly followed by the crash of a body hitting the hard ground. It was summer in Texas. We hadn't had rain in weeks. The temps had gotten as high as 101°. I knew that shit had to hurt.

By the time I had made it around the corner, I was greeted by Funky dragging the fat ass slob back in my direction. "That's a damn shame, Jesus. I just wanted to talk."

"Schina, I have known you for years. You never just want to talk. Not when you show up with him," he jerked his head in Funky's direction. He brought up a valid point, and I made a note to myself to start leaving his ass in the truck.

"Yea, you're right. But I was at least going to make it quick. Well as long as you told me what I wanted to know. Now you won't even get that mercy," I replied honestly. I looked Funky in the eye, before I turned to head back to my waiting truck. "Secure his ass in the truck. And from now on, you don't get out. Damn."

As we drove to Al's Pick N Pull, a junkyard where people could come and find car parts they needed, off of 2nd Avenue, I was banging to that Z-Ro *I Hate You Bitch*. Besides my kids, and the people in the Expedition caravan we had going on, the words to this song pretty much explained how I was feeling.

Music always seemed to mellow me out and I was hoping to calm down enough to ask Jesus the questions I desperately needed answers to. His answers would decide how many more stops I would have to make that night.

By the time we pulled in, and Funky had the gates open, ready for us to roll in, I thought myself to be calm enough to ask questions. I realized how wrong I was when we got to a corner far away from the road, and Funky had pulled Jesus' body from the truck. I immediately walked up and used all my force to punch him in his face.

"Where are my fucking kids, Jesus," I asked as blood squirted from his nose. I had hit him hard enough that if he lived, both eyes would be black. I didn't even give a fuck. The way I was feeling I doubted he was going to live anyway.

"What the hell are you talking about? I don't know where the girls are. Why would I know?" Due to the swelling in his face, his voice had gone nasal. I was so aggravated even that was annoying the fuck out of me.

"Because whoever took my fucking kids left a letter. The letter said since I took something from them, they took something from me. They also want five hundred thousand fucking dollars of *my* money. And... Well, I took your sister from you. And I also took your meal ticket, didn't I? I mean we all know Snake was your own personal ATM," I said aggressively.

"Man, you know I didn't give a damn about Bianca." By then, the nigga was crying. There wasn't anything I hated more than an ole soft ass nigga. "And Snake stopped giving me money when I got married."

If I took a moment to think about what he said, I'd have probably realized he was telling me the truth. Only problem was I was too far gone to think rationally.

"Well, here's our dilemma," I said calmly. My calmness spoke volumes on what was about to happen. "The text I received today came from your old stomping grounds. So I don't believe you. I swore to hunt down and kill any and everyone who may have had something to do with it. And right now you're at the top of the list. Since I always keep my word, yo ass gone die. But I'll send ya wife some money, though." The whole time we had been talking, Funky and Blue had been holding his ass still. "Tie his ass to that pole," I demanded, pointing to a telephone pole that was oddly placed in the middle of the junkyard.

Of course, by then Jesus was struggling, having come to realize I was serious. I waved my hand at Skeet and Chase to go help out. As they struggled, I went to the back of the Expedition I had arrived in and pulled out the new tool box of torture I had purchased. It was eleven and a half inches of black plastic. There were two layers and the top layer was detachable. Both layers had bright yellow tops. The top layer carried flat tools. But the bottom layer carried bigger, more fun tools.

I hadn't planned this event, so I opened both compartments and just stared at all the fun I had. The shiny scalpel caught my attention, but as I reached to grab it, I felt a sharp sting to my ankle. "What the fuck," I screeched. I looked to see what had caused the pain.

I was standing next to an ant pile. And not just any ants, fire ants. That's when my great idea hit. "Ivory I need you to run to the nearest store and grab a small," I looked at Jesus' overweight body. "Nah, make that a large jar of honey. Blue, take Skeet and Chris, and I want y'all to go talk to everyone we know in the East. I wanna know anyone we may have beef with over there. Anyone who may be acting funny. And I want to know by the time I open my eyes in the morning." Everyone was looking at me in confusion. "Just fucking go," I roared.

I watched as everyone scampered off to do what I asked. As the taillights disappeared, I decided to have a little fun. Just a little bit while I waited on Ivory to return. I reached into my toolbox and pulled out my scalpel. "Hey, Funky, you ever seen that movie with Nicolas Cage and John Travolta? Shit, what's the name of it? You know the one where John Travolta is the detective dude. Nicolas Cage is the criminal." The whole time I was speaking, I was staring at Jesus. I knew he knew what I was talking about. We had watched it together numerous times.

I watched as Funky did my signature move and rubbed his hands together. "Oh, man, if I know you like I think I do, this is about to get real interesting." Yea, he knew me as well as he thought he did.

"Schina," Jesus obviously also knew me very well, because I watched as a wet spot formed on the front of his shorts. "Please, don't do this."

"Well tell me who has my fucking kids," I roared angrily.

"Don't you think if I knew I would tell you," he pleaded as I inched closer to him. He was eyeing the shiny scalpel. I could see the fear in his eyes, if I was honest with myself, I'd admit that it turned me on.

"Well, I guess you gone fucking die in this bitch tonight. If you can't help me, I have no purpose for you." I meant every word I spat as I kept moving in his direction.

As I got within arm's reach of Jesus, I could see him flinch. He had been my friend for a very long time, so he knew it was about to get rough. I snaked my hand out and caressed his face, letting my hand linger on the soft double chins that jiggled with my touch.

"Ahhhhhh," he yelled as I made the first incision on his face. He continued to scream as I outlined his entire face with my scalpel. I was indeed about to take his face off.

I left the junkyard with a smile on my face. The only problems were, he didn't live as long as I had hoped. I had planned on covering him with honey and throwing him on the ant pile. He had always claimed to be allergic to fire ants, and I really wanted to see the reaction. Unfortunately, he bled out before Ivory made it back.

Chapter Eight
Bam

"Where are you going, Money?" I was sure my voice seemed to be extra whiny that day. I didn't even care. Damn, it had only been two days since his bitch of a wife had fucked me up. And while yea, Money had been by my side except for a couple hours that first day, I wanted him at home with me.

I knew I probably needed to be in someone's hospital, but for Money's sake, I had let the hood doctor come through instead. I knew in my heart though, that I would get a chance to exact my revenge.

"Man, I got shit to do. I been sitting here nursing your ass for two fucking days, Bam. Damn, call one of your friends over to sit with you or something." I knew right then that Money really didn't pay my ass any attention. I had barely talked to anyone since we hooked up, at least in his presence anyway.

"Baby, you know I don't kick it with anyone," I whined as I walked over to the dresser. He was just putting his cologne back and I realized I was losing the fight.

I did the one thing I thought would win. I tried to grab his dick. I figured the promise of some wet-wet would keep him home. My feelings were truly hurt when he just knocked my hands away.

"Look, babe," Money's voice sounded like he was about to spit some bullshit. Not even trying to hear what he was about to say, I started dragging my aching body back to my queen sized bed. I became even more frustrated as I almost tripped trying to kick shit out of my way.

"*Bitch, don't no man wanna woman who can't cook or clean,*" I heard my best friend's voice in my head as I climbed in the bed.

"Fuck you, hoe," I mumbled to her fading memory. She hadn't been gone long and I missed her every day. I shook her memory from my head as I noticed Money giving me a weird look.

"What you say, Paloma?" Ugh, he knew I hated that damn name. How my black ass mama gonna name me some Spanish shit?

"Don't call me that. And I didn't say anything to you. Just go ahead and give me whatever lame ass excuse you were about to give me," I said, trying to get his mind off the fact that I was slowly losing mine.

"I'm not about to give you an excuse," he said as he walked over to the bed. He was carefully following the trail I had just half ass made. I flinched as he used his index finger to trace one of the many bruises his bitch of a wife had left on my otherwise unblemished body.

"That hurts, boo," I complained. I purposely called him the pet name Schina had given him. That was my revenge for him calling me Paloma.

"I'm sorry, Bam. But like I was saying, I'm not just dropping an excuse off in ya lap. I know you heard Schina tell me I only have two weeks to stack as much bread as possible. Well, that's what I'm trying to do." I was disgusted at the thought of him being willing to let that bitch run him out of Dallas. At the moment, I was glad he was just a means to an end.

I guess my face showed my displeasure because he continued with his lame ass reasoning. "Just hear me out, love. I haven't even made up my mind on whether I am going to stay in Texas, go back to the Land, or relocate somewhere completely different. But no matter what choice, and especially if I decide to stay here and go to war with the Crew and them, I'm going to need as much cash on hand as possible. So while the getting is good, I need to be out there. Do you understand where I am coming from?"

The more he talked, the more annoyed I got. The more annoyed I got, the more I realized I was ready for the games to be over. The faster it was done, the faster I could be with my true love. That thought alone made me decide not to push the issue. Instead, I just nodded my head, which by then had begun to throb again. "Yea, I understand. Can you bring me a Pepsi and a pain pill before you leave?" Money nodded his head as he ran off to do as I asked.

After Money had been gone for a while, and the throbbing in my head had subsided, I decided to get up and take a shower. Before I could make it to the shower, XScape's *My Little Secret* began blaring from my phone. Excitedly, I skipped over to the night stand where my iPhone sat on the charger. I hated iPhones but Money insisted he wouldn't even use the same operating system as the crew. Now I was left with that piece of shit. *He could have at least gotten me the latest one*, I thought as I clicked answer.

"Hey," I answered in the sweetest voice I could conjure up at the moment.

"Hey gorgeous," the voice on the other end replied. "What's wrong with you? Why do you sound like that?"

Even though I had seen my love briefly the day I sent Money to the pharmacy and to get food, I was sure to cover my wounds. I made sure not to expose my heart to what had gone down. I wasn't sure if I had done it to keep them from acting out of emotion, or if I had hid it because I was embarrassed. But I had felt the need to hide it, nonetheless.

"Nothing, bae. I'm good," I responded in that same fake ass cheerful voice.

"Paloma Ayana Wilson, do not make me show up over there." I pulled my ear away from the phone as my future's voice got louder.

"What the fuck is up with everyone calling me by my government," I asked rhetorically as I headed into my bathroom. I sat on the toilet and looked around.

My bathroom was without a doubt the cleanest room in my house. Decorated in black, grey, and white, everything was in its place. The shelves that were above the toilet held my Bath & Body Works collection on the bottom. The middle shelves held neatly folded towels, following the color scheme of the room. And the top shelf held African sculptures and candles, also in black, white, and grey. My step-in garden tub was made of black marble and was surrounded by white candles of different fragrances. In the opposite corner was my shower. Hanging on the black matte rod next to the shower were white towels monogrammed with my initials. Between the toilet and tub was a his-and-hers countertop with two black marble sinks. All of the accessories on the counter were white and spotless. The walls were decorated with more African art done in black and white. Money always made jokes about me being so messy, except when it came to the one room no-one saw but he and I. I always just shrugged it off, though. I couldn't give a reason why.

"You know what, fuck this shit! I'm on my way." I had gotten so busy admiring my bathroom, I had forgotten all about the call I was on.

"No, no. I'm okay. Just think. If you get caught over here, it will ruin the whole plan. How would we explain your presence? But most important, how would we explain your physical condition? No, just stay at home and I will be by there in the next couple of days. Baby, stay with the plan."

"I hear you, Bam. If you aren't here the day after tomorrow, this plan gonna go down the drain. I promise I will bring my ass to your house. And when you come, bring some groceries." I could hear the seriousness in her voice.

"Okay, babe. I love you. I'll try to be there tomorrow, if not, the day after tomorrow at the latest. Send me a list of what kinda things you want from the store. I'm gonna take a bath and I'll talk to you later." *Click*. Well damn. I knew there was going to be trouble when the call was disconnected without an I love you, too. Oh well, there was nothing I could do about it at the moment. I decided to just shrug it off.

As I headed back into the bathroom, after placing my phone back on the charger, I grabbed a book off my shelf to enjoy while I was relaxing in the tub. Another thing I was very particular about was my books. On the top two shelves were books I had never read. While the books on the lower four shelves I had already enjoyed, or in some cases just read. I grabbed a book from the top shelf so I knew it was going to be a surprise. I pressed play on the remote that turned on the surround sound radio system. I was immediately enveloped by the crooning of Mary J. I absolutely loved me some heartbroken Mary. She would sing her heart out.

I went into the bathroom and turned the water on in the tub. I made sure to make it as hot as I could handle. I added some strawberry champagne bubble bath and began to strip off the panties and pink boy shorts I was wearing. I was fully prepared to enjoy that bath.

I must have fallen asleep in the tub because the next thing I knew I was being woke up to freezing cold water. That wasn't the scary part, though. The scary part was an angry Money standing over me. Not just standing over me, but holding my phone.

"Who is Shaw and why are they sending your mother fucking ass a grocery list?" I must have just stared at him stupidly for too long because he reached out and grabbed me by my hair. He was dragging my shivering body from the tub. Of course, I hadn't healed from the last ass kicking I had taken so I was in extreme pain.

"Stop Money," I screamed at the top of my lungs. I was hoping my neighbors would hear and call help, any help at that point, but I knew better. "I can explain, baby, just hear me out!"

"Well, you better," was the last thing I heard before everything went black.

Chapter Nine
Money

"Bruh, I know things are real fucked up right now," I had called the one person that I knew that was as close to my wife as they were to me. Blue.

"What you talking about, Money," he shot back. I figured he didn't think I knew he was working both sides of the fence. But it didn't take a genius to figure that shit out. I knew I hadn't bonded his ass out, so that only left the Queens. No-one else that Blue dealt with had that type of money to play with. Hell, I really didn't.

"Nigga, I know you still dealing wit' Schina n'em. I ain't even tripping on it. If I was you, I would be, too. That's why you are the person I need. I need some help, bruh"

There was a short pause that seemed to drag on forever, and then he sighed. "Bruh, I'ma just be straight up with you. If what you're about to ask me in anyway will cause drama or bring harm to the crew, you can count me out."

"Nigga, what? I wouldn't do that. But even if it was the plan, you were my boy. You moved to the D with me, not them hoes. You been my brother since the playground, nigga. How you just gonna walk away from that bond?" I hoped my voice didn't show the depth of the pain I felt in my heart right then. Just like I couldn't afford to lose any more of the people of my crew, I couldn't afford to show any more emotion.

"Yea, all that's true, my nigga. But you know what else? I ain't ever had to go sit in jail behind none of their shit either. I've never had to question their loyalty to the crew." I had to be tripping. I knew that nigga hadn't just told me that my loyalty to the crew had ever been under question.

"Cuz, what are you talking about? I may have fucked around on shawty, but I've always been true to the crew. Say what the fuck you mean dawg," I demanded.

"Nigga, we went to jail because you had to get ya dick wet. And that was just minutes after we picked up the package. How many missions have you rolled on? How many niggas you done slumped? And then when you answer that, think of what you were doing when the rest of us were putting in work." He let that sink in for a minute and then followed it up with, "Ain't nothing loyal about that, bro. Now tell me what you need and then I'll think about whether I'm willing to help ya ass."

I couldn't deny the fact that he had pissed me off, but before I could say anything about it, my wife's words resonated in my mind.

"The reason everyone shows me so much respect is because they know I won't hesitate to get out there and get dirty with them. Not to mention, boo, how many times have we had an emergency and yo ass was laid up with some random bitch?"

I pretty much kept hearing the same shit. And it was even crazier because I promised Schina and myself while we were in Mexico that I was going to do better. And then I thought of that video I had received, the one with images of my wife's legs being wrapped around someone else's neck. Shit, by then I knew I had overreacted. I could only hope the news I had for her would help me earn her trust back. That thought quickly brought me back to why I had even called Blue to begin with.

"I hear what you saying, bro. Maybe Schina will give me a chance to show her I realized how bad I fucked up, and maybe not. All I know is right now I have bigger issues," as I said that I glanced at trifling ass Bam. She was handcuffed to the headboard of her own bed. She had stopped the squirming she had been doing when I hit that hoe with a haymaker.

"Well, just spit it out, man, I got shit to do, and I don't have time for the riddles." I guess my brother from another mother really was tired of my shit. Once we handled this situation, I really needed to sit down and evaluate my life and the decisions I had made.

"I need you to get Schina to my house. I have information on who has the girls." *Click.* I stared at my phone and sure enough my screen flashed call disconnected. I stared at ole' girl one more time and shook my head. "You don't even know the consequences you have brought down on yourself."

***

Boom. Boom. Boom. I almost dropped the blunt I had just lit, when I heard the beating at the front door. I knew my wife was going to feel like I had something to do with it, so I was kinda nervous.

I drug myself to the front door. But before I even made it, I watched the door bust open, slamming into the wall behind it. I just shook my head. I should have seen that coming. I should have just left the damn door unlocked.

Of course, leading the pack was my wife, the head queen, as they called her. Shawty to me, though. I also saw she was still on her gangsta shit. She was wearing her damn gang colors and I was low key pissed off. Only thing that stopped me from commenting was I didn't want to feel her wrath, not any more than I was going to, anyway. So instead I just made eye contact with her, letting her read it in my face.

"Nigga, don't say shit to me about a mothafucking thing, unless it's about where my babies are." I was sure to the rest of the pack her voice was full of anger, but me, I could hear the defiance and pain. I knew then I had let her down for the last time.

"Just c'mon. I'll let Bam tell you about it herself. I didn't even let her tell me everything, just decided to wait for you."

"Nigga, you better not be wasting my fucking time. If you are, I swear I'ma leave you and that hoe in here stanking," her voice spoke of the truth in her words.

"Nah, when it came to something this serious, I wouldn't do that. C'mon, I got her ass tied up and waiting for y'all in the bedroom."

I watched Schina and Ivory share a look before Schina started leading everyone to the back of the house. Bam was obviously coming to because I could hear her moans. If she only knew I was easy and gentle on her ass. She thought I had caused her pain, but the Queens were undoubtedly about to teach her the true definition of the word.

I fell in line behind the crew that was following Schina. I hadn't really seen her in action in a long time and I was interested to see if she was still as sadistic as she used to be.

As I entered the bedroom behind everyone else, I heard a loud *whop*. I peeked around Funky Town's shoulder and saw that Bam had gotten her head rocked from side to side. I could only assume she had said something fly, but I hadn't heard anyone ask a question.

"Hoe, I know you wondering why I hit you and you ain't said shit." Okay maybe she hadn't said anything. "Well I hit yo' ass cuz I want you to know upfront that I am not playing with your ass. I heard you have information on where my children are and I want it now! So I suggest yo' ass get to muhfucking talking, hoe."

Chapter Ten
Bam

What the fuck had I gotten myself into? I had to sit back and wonder if it was even worth the drama, but then I thought of Bianca, my best friend of over fifteen years. I realized no matter how this turned out, yes, it was worth it. I thought of the pain and anger that probably shot through Money's heart when he saw the video of his precious wife creeping. I thought of the pain her best friend must have felt sitting by her side while she was laid up in Parkland. And finally, I thought of the pain Schina's bitch ass had probably felt every second of every day since she woke up, having no idea where her darling daughters were. No matter what the outcome was, knowing I had inflicted such pain on them was well worth it.

"Bitch, I ain't telling your ass shit. You just gone have to figure it out your damn self," I said defiantly.

"Grab that hoe. We gone take her ass to the house off Martin Luther King. Y'all put her in y'alls truck," she said looking at the three menacing looking men that were standing behind her. "Money, you gone ride with me and Ivory. Bring yo' pistol, too, nigga, if you even still have one." Even I could hear the mockery she was making of his gangsta. I couldn't help but to laugh.

All heads turned in my direction when they heard me laughing. It was the fat ass white girl who decided to address it, though. "What the fuck is so funny? Nah, you know what, you ain't even gotta answer. You should save all of your breath for the screaming I'm sure your dumb ass is about to do." She turned and started walking out the door. I heard her mumble something about how dumb hoes always wanna test the wrong ones.

As the handcuff that was around the bed post was removed and shackled to my free wrist, I couldn't help but to think of my best friend. Bianca had been by my side for so much. When I lost my baby, she was the one who sat by my side at the hospital. When my baby Shawn was shot by that crazy ass bitch, Bianca was the one who comforted me. I would forever hate the bitch for taking my sister from me.

I knew it was Schina who had killed Bianca because we were on the phone discussing her issues with Money when Schina and her pack of followers had pulled up in her driveway.

I hadn't even realized I was crying until the nigga who was toting my ass stated, "I don't really see the point in crying now. Y'all bitches kill me. Y'all always wanna go off half-cocked, acting off of emotion, and then when the consequences come to bite you on the ass, y'all wanna start that sniveling and crying shit." He shook his head as he entered the living room. As he turned the corner, he managed to let my head bounce off the wall.

I refused to scream or acknowledge the pain that rocked through my brain. Fuck them. I knew from word around town that Schina got off on pain, and even though she was already out of the front door, I still wasn't going to give her that pleasure.

"Nigga, here, throw this blanket over her ass before you walk out the door. I don't see anyone outside, but we don't want anyone seeing yo' big ass tote this butt naked ass bitch outside," the shorter of the three niggas that were left in the house with me said. I watched him grab the Dallas Cowboys throw blanket that was spread across the back of my couch. I then felt it as he tossed it over my body.

I tried to think of a way to get out of this situation. I only had a few minutes because Martin Luther King wasn't that far away from my house. Judging from the force in which I was tossed in the back of the truck, though, I probably didn't have much chance in flipping anyone. Well at least not the do as she says ass nigga that had begun to tie my ass into the truck. They had some kind of car seat contraption built in. I took it that the Expedition was used on missions like this. It was a smart move, too.

If I would have been given a chance, my naked ass would make a run for it.

I was left facing the back doors of the truck, so I couldn't see them all climb into the front seats. I did vividly hear all the doors slam. Due to the pain in my body, I could feel every vibration the truck gave off as it was started and started pulling off into the street.

I tried to think of a way to maybe pull at least one of these niggas over to me and bae's side, but to be honest, I knew her crew was too damn loyal to play that game with me. Everyone knew Money was the weakest link when it came to the crew, and we see how that turned out for me. So instead of even trying it, I just thought about some of the best times I had had with my bestie, Bianca.

I remembered the day she called and told me she had met the man of her dreams. *"Oh my God, Bam, you have to meet this new nigga that Snake is supplying. He's so fucking fine. And he's the head of his own crew. Nigga came all the way from Cleveland and shut all these Dallas niggas down. I heard his crew be putting in work."*

I had a sinking feeling in my stomach when I heard that. Lord, please don't let her be talking about that nigga, Money. *"Bitch, please, please tell me you ain't talking about that nigga, Money. You're talking about his right-hand man, Blue, right?"*

"Bitch, how you know them?" I swear the girl could be dense as hell.

"Girl, their names are ringing all through Dallas. That nigga, Money, has a woman though."

"C'mon, bestie, you know damn well I don't care about him having a woman. I don't have no problem snatching a nigga out from under his woman." That was the one thing I really couldn't stand about Bianca. I continuously told her that shit was going to catch up with her.

And it did. I wished I would have known back then how detrimental it would be. I'd have fought harder to get her to leave that nigga where he was, with his crazy ass wife.

As I stared out the back window and realized we had just turned onto Martin Luther King, I came to the disturbing conclusion that I was probably about to meet my best friend in the afterlife. I could only hope they never found out who bae was. I was hoping she could pull off the rest of the plan. At least my death wouldn't be in vain.

As we pulled into a driveway of some house on a rundown street, I thought back to the last conversation I had with Bianca. But even more than our conversation, I remembered listening to her die, and how painful it sounded.

"Bitch, I can't believe you would give that nigga's dope to the one man he truly has hatred for," I expressed to Bianca after hearing her tell me how she had given DB Money's package.

"Yea, but I bet that nigga will think twice before he puts his hands on a bitch like me again," was the best reply she could come up with. *"I mean, he's locked up now, what can he do to me?"*

I had sighed as I thought about how ugly the situation was about to get. At that moment, neither of us knew that death was already in route to her. "I keep telling you that Money isn't the one you need to worry about. You had already called the law on the man. Your ass should have just left it at that, but you always gotta be extra." I lit a Newport as I tried to think of a way to help my best friend.

"Maybe we can go get the package back from DB. Even if Money is going to be in jail for a long time, there is no doubt in my mind that he's going to send his psycho ass wife after his drugs, hoe."

"I wish that hoe would..." Her voice had trailed off and I could hear rustling in the background. She was the only person

I knew who still used a plain old Bluetooth device. That shit made everything she did loud as hell in my ear.

"What the hell are you doing, B," I asked her.

"Bitch, you done talked them hoes up. Schina and her two pussy lickers are at my gate. Damn, that was quick. I wonder how she figured out where I was?" I had been telling her for months that the Queens had eyes and ears every damn where. Only problem was she had a bad habit of only thinking with her pussy. "I'm about to go out here and see what they want. I'ma call you back."

Before I could protest, she had disconnected the call. I decided to give her five minutes and then I was calling her ass back. Even if she was in denial about how those chics gave it up, I wasn't. I decided to go put some clothes on just in case I needed to hurry over there.

As soon as I slipped on my last shoe, I grabbed my phone and called Bianca back. I heard the beep of the call being connected but instead of hearing Bianca say hello, I was greeted by a voice I recognized very well. Schina.

"Bitch, don't even start. There is nothing you can say to make this better. I appreciate you always trying to save my relationship. But this time he has risked everything we have worked so hard for behind this nasty ass girl. Just hand me my tool kit."

Fuck, I knew what that meant. I wasn't sure what had gone down in the time that I was off the phone, but obviously things weren't about to end well. I grabbed my keys and sprinted out of my house, but it was a forty-five minute drive to the house B had chosen to hole up in. I probably wasn't going to make it in time, but I damn sure had to try.

I heard some rustling in the background and I almost decided to just hang up and call DPD. I could just send them over there to handle it. Only thing was I knew if I did, Schina would have

Dallas after not only me, but my entire family. My best bet was to ignore the speed limit and try to get my ass there.

As I hit the highway, I heard one of the most sinister sentences ever. It made my blood freeze. "Oh yea, I'm about to have fun with your slut ass."

That day I was pretty much forced to listen to the screams of my best friend as she met her demise as she was killed by the hands of that sick fuck. I listened to the crackle of fire before the flames overtook her phone and disconnected our call. I also swore that day that I would make her ass hurt, too. If I had to die in the process, then so-be-it.

As the back doors were snatched open, I looked upwards to the heavens and mouthed, "Here I come, B."

Chapter Eleven
Nicole

"Damn, where is my Boosie C.D.? Can you look in that C.D holder over your mirror," I asked the person sitting in the passenger seat of my 2015 red Chevy Camaro. I stared at his sexy ass and wondered if fucking with him was going to be worth the drama. I knew it was going to cause drama between me and my girls. That much I knew. As I thought of the way he laid the pipe down, yea, I knew it was worth it.

"Here you go, Nikki," he said as he handed me the C.D. I had asked for. I knew I was feeling him way more than I should have been, because no-one had been allowed to call me Nikki since the death of my father. "Now you never told me where we were heading? So what's on our agenda for the day?"

I stared at him, and fell a little bit more in love with him. I loved the way he just let me lead. He didn't ask a lot of questions and, even though he was a boss in his own right, he never questioned the moves I made. Hell, he seemed to believe in me more than the other Queens. The crew was so far up Schina's ass, they questioned any directives that didn't come straight from her mouth.

"I gotta go to the main house and count up the stash. I have to make sure the count is right. You know Jorge ain't playing no games. And the way Schina has even him wrapped around her finger, I'm sure I would be the only one to pay any consequences if this shit ain't right."

"I been told your ass, quit trusting these niggas. You need to count their drops as soon as they hand it to you. Quit believing that everything is going to turn out right. If you really feel that way about my dad, then you need to be more concerned with self-preservation."

Yea, I was riding with that nigga, Blacc, and I felt no guilt in my heart. Ivory wasn't my girl, that was Schina's best friend. The way I saw it, all was fair in love and war. I knew I couldn't win a war against the Crew, but I didn't think Schina would let no personal shit like this cause a war to break out. I was sure she would just let me and Ivory handle this one-on-one, at least that's what I kept telling myself.

Blacc had gotten out two weeks ago, but because Ivory was so stuck up Schina's ass, she had missed his call. Since then, their relationship had been unraveling. I knew they both cared about each other, but she hadn't handled her responsibilities as a woman. I mean, everyone knows, if yo nigga been on lock, it's your job to be popping pussy as much as possible.

"Yea, I hear you, B, but the crew got most of these niggas so shook, it ain't ever been an issue," was all I could think to respond.

"Yea, but, it ain't the crew making pick-ups and drop-offs no more. It's just you and the two dudes my dad left down here to help out, at least until all the drama blows over. A lot of niggas are going to notice that the key players aren't showing their faces. Eventually, someone is going to test the waters. Mark my words, lil mama."

I knew what he was saying was true, but really I ain't have time to be counting each pick-up every damn time. So what I did instead was give each trap house a money bag with a specific symbol on it. Then I would count each one and if anyone was short I would know exactly which house it was. Blacc knew this already, so I didn't even know why we had to keep going through the same ole shit.

"I hear you. I don't even wanna discuss it no more. Let's just get over here and count this money up so I can hand that shit off to Antonio," I said, speaking of the newest guy that Jorge, our connect and Blacc's dad, had sent down here to help. "After we get through with that, I figured we could grab something to eat and head to my house for a while."

And just like I figured, the idea of some of this wet-wet made him shut the hell up. As he nodded his head, I reached over and turned up the volume on Boosie. All I wanted to do was ride and jam on the way to the house on Audelia in Garland. I had to give it to Schina, the chances of her ever taking a major loss were slim to none. If it happened, it would have to be one of the Queens or one of those crazy ass niggas she kept by her side. Her shit was spread all over the damn metroplex. The main dope house was all the way out in Ft. Worth. I didn't even have access to that shit.

Whenever I needed packages to do drop offs, I had to call some bitch who called herself White Shadow. I hated calling her for two reasons. One, the bitch gave me the creeps. She literally made my skin crawl every time I was in her presence. And two, where did this hoe come from that she was more trusted with the stash than my ass. I ain't see her white ass risking her life and freedom for the crew, year after year. But, oh well, I would deal with that at a later date. We had finally pulled up to the count house and I was just ready to get that shit out of the way.

As I killed the engine on my car, I noticed a black Navigator pull in behind me. I couldn't see through the windshield but I was pretty sure it was Antonio and whatever Mexican he had with him for today's count. I didn't really understand why they had to be around for the count, it's not like they actually counted a damn thing. Antonio usually stood around on the phone chatting in Spanish to some unknown person.

"Fuck. Let's get this shit over with," I sighed as we exited my car and headed up the cobblestone sidewalk to the two story cream colored house. I had actually fallen in love with this house and was hoping to one day turn it into my permanent residence.

It was a beautiful house. It had a perfectly manicured lawn that led up to a spacious porch. It even had a swing connected to the ceiling. It had double doors that were red and had oval shaped glass inserts. Once you entered the doors you were immediately greeted by beautiful hardwood floors and all-white everything else. To the left of the hallway was a kitchen with an eat-in nook. There were all white appliances and the fridge was huge. Directly across from that was a formal dining room. Even though no one lived here, it was fully furnished and the dining room held all white furniture that popped against the dark floors. Down the corridor, the hall expanded into a gigantic living room that also boasted all white furniture, including the baby piano in the corner. The back wall was all glass and was covered with white sheer curtains. To the left of the room was a sprawling staircase that led to the three bedrooms upstairs. Each of those bedrooms had their own bathrooms attached. The master had no walls and all windows. Yes, one day I wanted to make this my house.

"Every time we walk in this house you get a star struck look on your face," I was brought back to the task at hand by Blacc's soothing voice. "How long do you think it will be before she places this one on the market?"

I didn't know, so I just shrugged my shoulders and toted the duffle bag I was carrying into the formal dining room. As I dumped bag after bag of money onto the beautiful table, I let my mind think about how Schina had the stash houses set up. It had always been the same. One thing only a few people knew was that Schina owned a real estate company. She rarely sold a house though, only rented. Every time a renter would move, whichever stash house had been in the same spot for the longest would relocate to the newly empty house. The former stash house would get a thorough cleaning, and would then be placed on the market. If I was in the mood to give credit, I would say it's a genius move, but I wasn't feeling nice at the moment.

***

Four hours had passed and we had just got through counting the money for the second time. The first time using money counters and the second time by hand. I was still in denial and I really wanted to count this shit all over again, but I knew that it was a reality. I also knew I couldn't call on Schina, because when I tried to call her about a smaller and much less important issue, she had snapped, told me to handle that shit like she was still in the hospital. I had almost gotten pissed off, but I knew how deep her love for her children was. I also realized she wasn't in her right frame of mind.

"Fuck." There were no words strong enough to convey the anger that I was feeling. "It's always some shit with them South Dallas niggas, man."

"Well, the only thing to do now is handle it. So what you gone do?" I was so damn angry even the sound of Blacc's voice was pissing me off.

I just glared at him. I guess he didn't know how the Queens got the fuck down. I may not have been rolling with Schina and Ivory like before, and I may have been doing some ol' trifling shit by fucking with his tired ass, but I was still a Queen in my own damn right.

"I don't know why you looking at me like that. I ain't done shit to you. I'm on your side."

"Well, if you really on my side, strap up, nigga. The streets about to bleed. Nobody plays with my money." I felt like I shouldn't have even had to answer that question, but since I did, I kept it as simple as possible.

***

It hadn't been an hour since I noticed the short money and I already had a truck full of niggas. They were all ready to cause chaos with me. Of course, it wasn't the niggas I was used to roll-ing with, considering they were all rolling with Schina, but those fools were just as crazy.

Blacc was driving and I was seated behind him. Sitting in the passenger seat was this dude from Singing Hills named Tye. Tye had just got out of Huntsville, one of Texas's ratchet ass prisons, and he was trying to support his wife, LeeLee, their two children, and their bad ass Chihuahua. When he came to me and asked to be put down with the crew, I immediately looked him up. His background seemed pretty solid and I learned quickly that he took no shit. Because of that, he was invited, not only into the crew, but into my own circle of killers. I had to admit LeeLee had her a sexy ass man. He was six feet two inches tall, the color of caramel, dark brown eyes, and he still carried his prison mus-cles. Tye stayed dressed in all black. I could only assume it was that stay ready mentality. Like I said, dude was fine.

Sitting beside me was a dude named James. James was from Florida. He hadn't been in Texas long, but he had already proven himself to be a gangsta. The day I met the five foot eight inch white haired white boy I was coming out of Rainbow corner store on Beckley. I saw a group of four teenage boys preying on his ass. It seemed like he was strolling down the cut paying no at-tention to his surroundings and I just knew he was about to get his shit snatched, possibly his life. I pondered for a short amount of time whether I should get involved, deciding to just sit back and watch the show.

Just as the boys got within five feet of the white boy, I watched him spin on his loafers. He all of a sudden became the predator. He was aiming what I knew to be a .357 at the biggest of the teenagers. That wasn't what sold me on his crazy ass, though. It was when he said, "Hood law says if I pull my heat, I have to use it." And then he let that thing bark. I immediately knew I had to have him on the squad. He had been rocking with me since.

As I looked around me, I knew I had the right crew. It was time to go handle these sticky finger ass niggas. What they ain't know was they were about to unass my money and their spirit. I wanted everything that was owed to me.

Chapter Twelve
Schina

"Look at this hoe," I said pissed the hell off. "Praying and shit. I promise there's not a God anywhere, in any galaxy, in any dimension that's going to save your ass."

I watched as Money snatched her ass out of the truck. I couldn't help but to look at my husband and miss him. He was so fucking sexy, even when I was pissed at him. I hadn't laid next to him in a little over a month, hadn't kissed his pretty ass lips, and hadn't hugged his broad manly shoulders. We had been through so much bullshit together, but if I was honest with myself not only did he still make my heart skip a beat, he still made my panties wet.

I shook my head as I was grabbed from my Money lusting daze. This bitch was screaming like a damn fool. Just as I reached out to slap her silly ass, my husband beat me to it, with a swift punch to the ribs. Yea, that shit was turning me on. This was the nigga I met, before all the hoes took over. I adored take charge gangsta ass Money, too bad it was too late for us. I just couldn't see me getting over the fact that his ass was nowhere to be found while our daughters were missing. And then to find out he was sleeping with the enemy, whether he knew it or not, that was just too damn much for me.

"Take that bitch in the basement," I made the demand of Money like he didn't know what was about to take place. This house had one purpose. I liked to call it my torture chamber. Each room was sound-proofed except the living room, and each room had its own purpose. I had been wanting to take someone through the whole course of the house, but no-one ever lasted long enough to get a full tour. I was just hoping this bitch kept playing tough that way she could at least see each room. I didn't see that shit happening, but anything was possible.

"I got you, shawty," he answered as he slung her over his shoulder and entered the steel enforced door we had installed a few months ago. The last thing I needed was the laws running up in here. It wasn't really a concern of mine. I had added a couple of agents and detectives to the payroll while I was still laid up, unable to do any real work. I couldn't just leave everything to Ivory and them, so I expanded our connections.

As we walked towards the basement, I pulled out a burner phone and called that nigga, Blue. I had him on another mission at the moment. "Hey, how are things going?"

"Well, actually, I can't seem to find ya mama anywhere. There's just no sign of her."

I scratched my head with the barrel of Bonnie, the name I had given the .50 I was holding in my left hand. I was so glad I was taught how to shoot with both hands, cuz I hated busting one gun without the other.

"A'ight. Just stay on it. She has to be somewhere. I'll call you a little later and see if anything changed. Right now I'm about to have a little fun. Make sure everyone knows there's a reward for info on my mama." I disconnected the call and dropped the phone on the ground and stomped it.

I thought I had been talking fairly quiet, but I realized I hadn't been when I saw Money whip his head in my direction as he waited for Funky to unchain the basement door. "Who the fuck you talking to, Schina?"

I snapped my head quickly from left to right. I knew the nigga didn't call himself checking me about who the hell I was talking to. Not while he was carrying the bitch he had been laid up with while my crew looked for our children. "First off, nigga, you have no damn right to worry about who the fuck I'm talking to." I pointed my gun at the bitch that was now struggling against his hold. "The only bitch you can question right now is that dumb hoe. But I tell you what, if I'm feeling generous, after my kids are home, I'll let you ask whatever you want to as you pack your shit and get it the fuck out of my house."

He had Raschina Marie Morgan fucked all the way up. "How this nigga gone have the audacity to ask me about a mothafucking thing and I'm about to put this work on another one of his hoes? Another one. Where the fuck they do that at? Someone please enlighten my ass. I must be simple or some shit, cuz I'm damn sure not understanding." I was looking around at everyone in the room, waving my pistol in the air, hoping someone, okay not someone, hoping Money's dumb ass would say some shit. I was too damn close to the edge. Between the pregnancy hormones, my kids missing, and not to mention we still hadn't addressed the fact that this nigga had put his fucking hands on me.

Whack! I didn't even realize I had moved in Money's direction until I watched his body hit the ground. As he hit the ground, he caused that bitch Bam to go down with him. I looked around wildly for a chair. Each room had a chair placed directly in the middle of the room, because, well everyone knows how death makes my juices flow.

But this time I didn't need it for that reason. I was suddenly lightheaded and I realized my baby needed me to calm down. "Y'all quit staring at me like y'all don't know what time it is. Someone tie that dumb bitch up. Actually, strap her to that gurney," I said, pointing to a regulation gurney. I just happened to have a paramedic friend with a bad coke problem. He got me all kind of shit. "But tie her ass up face down. Ivory, I need you to go to McDonalds and get me the twenty piece nugget meal and two large Sprites. Make sure to get extra honey mustard and sweet n' sour sauce."

I watched my best friend as she shook her head and mumbled about me being an old greedy, coldhearted bitch, but she didn't question me. She just walked out to do as I asked. I didn't know what I would do without her, and I really needed to do something special for her. Maybe I would buy her mama that house she had been begging Ivory for. I didn't know what to do for her, but I would figure it out when shit calmed down.

"What you want us to do with Money," Chance asked as he was about to bend down and pick Money up. I had never really paid attention to his dominating size, not until I realized he probably could pick up Money like it wasn't shit. That was one huge ass dude.

"Leave that hoe ass nigga right there," I said, pointing to where they had shoved his body when they pulled his latest conquest out from under him. "That negro'll come to eventually. I ain't hit his punk ass that damn hard." I couldn't help but to look at his ass in disgust. And to think I was just getting wet thinking about him. It suddenly became more than clear to me that things between Money and I would never be repaired. There was no way to heal all of the hurt that had taken place over the last ten years.

"A'ight, she's tied down, boss lady," Chance's right hand Chase said to me. I could see the excitement in his eyes. They knew how I worked and they knew things were about to get very interesting.

I hauled myself up from the chair, even though I had just gotten comfortable. The lightheaded feeling had passed so I could get the party started while I waited on my food. I walked over to a steel cabinet and opened the two double doors. I pondered over the tools hanging there. I had a belt covered with metal studs, some garden shears, and a mini torch. There were also some medieval torture devices I had paid handsomely for. There was the breast ripper, designed to rip the breasts from women. I had a cattle prod, a tongue tearer, and my favorite, something called the tucker telephone. The tucker telephone connected from one wire on the person's big toe to their genitals. In this case, it would be her nipples. These wires connected to a crank on the far wall and when cranked, the person would receive electric shock from everything between their toes and genitals.

I grabbed the tucker telephone and the belt before walking over to a smaller cabinet that was sitting directly next to the larger one. When you opened this cabinet you would swear I was about to film some sort of BDSM porn movie. But, nope, these toys would in no way inflict pleasure, even though that's what they had been intended for. I didn't even ponder my decisions in this cabinet, simply grabbing the eighteen inch double headed dildo that had been specially equipped with shock wires and the matching anal plugs.

As I walked towards my newest and most important victim, I wondered how long it would take her to talk. While I wanted to know right then where my children were, I also wanted to have fun with her ass. I mean, who the fuck did she think she was, to not only take my kids but also to call herself shacking up with my fucking husband. Even if I didn't want him at the moment, he was still *my* fucking husband.

I set all of my tools on a table a few feet away from the gurney she was on. I reached over and pulled the gurney further away from the wall. I was going to need some room. After I got her into the position I wanted her in, I realized Chase had gagged her. While this is normally something I would require, today I needed to be able to hear every word uttered, so I unclasped it and tossed it to the floor.

"So, bitch," I said as I squatted in front of her face, "we can do this the easy way and you can just tell me where the fuck my kids are, or I can make this shit very painful."

"Bitch, fuck you. Yo' ass gone hurt just like I did when you took my best friend from me." I barely moved fast enough as she tried to spit on me. I didn't even take a moment to try to figure out who her bitch ass best friend was before I walked over to the table and grabbed the belt. I was glad the hoe was already naked. I didn't have to waste any energy cutting her shit off.

"You a nasty hoe, huh?" I didn't even give her a chance to reply as I swung the belt with all my might, letting the metal studs thud against her skin. I stood back and admired the blood that was already pooling on her skin. Just as I lifted my hand to swing again, I happened to look over and see that Money had come to. I turned my head to look directly in his eyes as I swung again. *Whomp, whomp, whomp*, the belt thudded against her skin as I swung repeatedly. Surprisingly, he never flinched as she screamed loud enough to burst ones ear drums.

I crooked my finger at him as I finally stopped swinging the belt. Amidst her screams, which hadn't ended with my swings, he pulled himself up and headed in my direction. He was leaving small speckles of blood on the floor as he semi staggered in my direction. As he made it over to me, I continued to maintain eye contact, trying to read any sympathy for his pussy trap. If I would have spotted any, he would have been tied to the gurney beside hers.

"What is it, Raschina," he asked with an even voice. He didn't even realize he had likely just saved his own damn life. Instead of replying, I simply grabbed his face and stuck my tongue down his throat. I moaned as I relished a taste I had once been so familiar with. His mouth always tasted like a mixture of Kush and peppermints.

As I pulled back, I took a moment to reach down and grab his semi hard dick. I resisted the urge to twist it and instead simply handed him the belt in my hands. "Well, it's too late for you to earn Dallas. This is now my shit. But the least you can do is handle this lil ole situation. Make that bitch tell you where my kids are. And if you can't get the information you will join that hoe and whoever she was crying about in the deepest darkest pits of hell, my nigga."

Knowing my niggas weren't going to let him do shit to me, I turned my back on him and headed back to my chair. I didn't think Money had ever seen the effects that death had on me, but he was damn sure going to find out that day.

Chapter Thirteen
Money

I should have known by the glances all the niggas in the room shot each other that shit was about to get even crazier. But I didn't have time to contemplate what was about to happen because I was trying to stay alive. I had no doubt that she would kill my ass right along with Bam.

"Baby, you just gonna let her tell you what to do?" I knew Bam was just using any tactic she thought would make me spare her life, but that shit went in one ear and out the other.

"Just tell me who has the girls and where they are and we can make this a lot quicker," she was answered by Schina before I could even begin to form an answer.

"Fuck you, hoe. When you killed Bianca, I swore to myself that you would feel my pain, and now you do. I'll just have to die today." I stared into her eyes that spoke of the true pain and fear that she felt. I was blown away. What the fuck did Bianca have to do with any of this?

Obviously, I had missed something because Schina didn't even sound surprised as she burst into laughter. "Oh, I guess that's the best friend you was hollering about before your nasty ass tried to spit on me. Well, don't worry, hoe. Before the day is over, you'll be reunited with that cum bucket ass slut. Money, handle your business. Fuck what she talking about."

I had never been into the torture shit so I turned around. I was meaning to ask her exactly what the hell she wanted me to do with all of this shit she had piled on this table, but I was in shock when I turned around and noticed Schina removing her pants. "What the fuck, Schina?"

I was irritated when all of the men in the room started chuckling. "Damn, nigga, you ain't know death turns your woman on?" I turned to Funky with a look of confusion on my face. He just continued to laugh before he said anything else. "That's a fucking shame, my nigga, and it says a lot about your relationship. Or lack of, anyway."

I immediately let my mind drift back to that day at the mall, when I saw the look of lust in her eyes after she shot Shawn. Yea, it all made sense. "That shit is ridiculous," I muttered under my breath.

"Nigga, don't worry about what the fuck I'm doing. What you need to be trying to do is preserve your own fucking life. I'm not going to tell you again to handle your fucking business, Byron."

I just shook my head as I finally grabbed the extra-large dildo on the table. As I grabbed it, I noticed that it had some loose wires hanging from one end. "What the fuck is this shit man?"

Schina giggled before she answered, so I turned to look at her sick ass. My wife was actually sitting there rubbing her clit as she laid her head back. "Just insert the end with the wires into, well whatever part of her body you want to, and then watch the fun."

I watched her rub her pussy some more, feeling my dick brick up, and then I turned to do what she said. "Look, Bam, why you don't just tell me who Shaw is and where she is so we ain't gotta go through all this extra shit?" I was almost begging. This wasn't my kind of thing, and I could admit that I wasn't entirely comfortable.

"I ain't telling y'all shit." I guess she was tougher than my ass, or else she hadn't really heard all the rumors of the shit my wife did to people who stood against her.

Knowing that the tides were going to turn, I hurried and shoved the end of the dildo up her pussy. I shoved it until I couldn't shove it any further. The scream that emitted from her mouth was enough to make me never want to go against the crew in any way. I wasn't exactly sure what was going on, but I knew it couldn't be good.

"You know what, this nigga ain't cut out for this shit," I heard behind me. "Funky, handle that shit for him. But he gets a pass for now. He at least fucking tried. Ol' soft ass nigga."

I knew I had to try to man the fuck up, but if I was being honest with myself, seeing this side of my wife had me feeling some type of way. "What you ain't gone do is keep disrespecting me, Schina. Regardless of where the fuck I rest my head, I am still your god damn husband and you will respect me as such." I made sure to add some bass to my voice as I looked her eye to eye. I had no idea what her reaction to what I just said was going to be, and I really ain't give a fuck. I was still a man, and my woman was going to treat me as such.

Surprisingly, she just nodded her head and told me to move my ass out the way. Accepting what she was willing to give at that moment, I did what she asked, moving to stand behind her chair, but trying to keep my eye on that crazy ass nigga, Funky. I remembered when we were in Mexico and we went to the Museum of Medieval Torture. All she could talk about was how much that fool would have enjoyed it. Judging from the look on his face as he realized he was up to bat, I believed her.

Before he could get started, we all could hear the latch on the basement door. Click. Click. Click. Click. Click. Click. All you could hear was five guns getting ready to blast whatever unfortunate fool was about to descend those stairs. Everyone had pulled a gun with the exception of Schina, and of course Bam.

"Y'all put the damn guns up. It's just Ivory. I can smell my chicken nuggets from here." I, too, could smell the food, but I wasn't dropping my gun until all of them dropped theirs.

"It is just me, y'all, and I'm alone. It's all good. Proceed." Evidently that was all that they needed to hear, because everyone returned their guns to wherever they pulled them from and Funky turned back towards Bam. He grabbed the dildo out of her pussy but she kept whimpering. I made a note to ask Schina what the fuck that shit was, but right then, I was more interested in what was about to take place.

I watched shawty as she pinched her nipples, which I knew was something she did when she was anticipating good sex. I had seen it too many times right before we had make-up sex. I then watched as that big ass nigga carried the dildo over to the table and picked up a butt plug that had the same kind of wires hanging from the end.

"See if the hoe is ready to talk before you cause her any more pain," Schina said to him as he was in mid-stride.

But before he could even say anything, Bam managed to force out, "I'm still not saying shit."

"That's fine wit' me, hoe. I wanna bust this fucking nut any-way. I didn't get to bust with the last nigga I killed, cuz dude bled out too fucking fast, so I'm going to enjoy this shit. You'll talk eventually. And if you don't, I'll kill your whole fucking fam-ily." The calmness in her voice was almost scary. I couldn't be-lieve I had slept next to a damn psychopath for all those damn years, but it was also turning me on, and that made me even more confused.

"Bitch, do you want these nuggets?" Everyone in the damn room had problems. Ivory was waving the McDonalds bag at Schina like she didn't have one hand on her nipples and one hand on her fucking pussy, and Schina was just waving her away like all of this was normal. But I guessed for them it was.

For hours, I sat and watched the mother of my only child masturbate as her handpicked partners in crime took turns tortur-ing the woman I had been laying with for the last month. She never asked me to join in the rotation, and I couldn't say that I blamed her. I didn't even know what half the shit that they pulled out was called, much less what the hell it did, or how to use it.

All I know is that by the end of the night, I had heard screams of pain that I was sure I would never get out of my head. I also knew I had heard my shawty scream in pleasure three damn times. But through all of that, Bam never gave up her accomplice.

***

Later that night as I climbed out of the shower, I heard my phone ringing. I rushed out of the bathroom and grabbed it off of the dresser, noticing that it was shawty. "What is it, shawty?" I really didn't have anything to say to her, and I was hoping she didn't have anything to say to me either, but she obviously did.

"Come open the door." I couldn't imagine why she was there, but I wrapped a towel around my waist and went to let her in. "Hey, boo," she said as I opened the door.

Hey boo, I thought as I stepped back so that she could enter the house. I stuck my head out the door and peeped the neighborhood before I shut and locked the door behind us. "Since when am I boo again, and what are you doing here, alone at that?"

"You're always going to be my boo, no matter what happens between us. And I didn't think I needed a reason or an entourage to come visit my own damn husband." I just stared at her and she laughed that angelic laugh that I honestly missed. "Yea, that shit ain't even sound right did it?"

"Nah, ma, so cut the bullshit and tell me why you're really here. And how the hell you got away from Ivory ass."

"Well, I came to get some dick. And we need to talk. I didn't really get away from Ivory she had Skeet follow me over here. I'm supposed to tell you that if you let anything happen to me tonight she will cut your balls off and feed your ass to Delgado." While she was saying it, I could hear a hint of laughter in her voice, but I knew that she was speaking the truth. I also knew that Ivory would at least try.

"Well, I was about to have some nachos and smoke a blunt, you wanna join me?"

"Hell, yea. My high yella' ass is hungry." I handed her a bag of weed and some cigars as I headed into the kitchen to make the nachos. As I got our plates ready and made two glasses of sweet tea, I heard her turn the radio on. Just my fucking luck the first song to play was Lauryn Hill's *Ex-Factor*. I was hoping that she would change it, but as soon as I heard her start crooning, I knew that wasn't going to happen. I just hoped it didn't make her want to fight.

"Here, shawty," I said, setting the plate and glass of tea down on the coffee table in front of her. Before I went back to get my own plate, I turned the radio off and the television on.

"What are you doing, Money," she whined in response. "I was listening to that."

"Yea, I know. That's exactly why I turned that shit off. I don't know why your mood towards me is so pleasant right now, but that shit wasn't gone do shit but ruin it. Fuck all that." I grabbed my food and rushed back to the living room before she had a chance to turn the radio back on. To my surprise, when I returned, she was sitting there stuffing her face. "Damn, slow down, shawty. Ain't nobody gone take yo' shit." I laughed as she seemed to eat faster.

"Shut up, Money. I'm hungry as fuck. It's like my ass just can't get full." It seemed that way, too, because her ass finished her plate and half of mine.

As we were smoking one of the blunts she had rolled, it really struck me that she said she came over for some dick. I wasn't about to fuck her in this dead bitch's house. I was only still here because I planned on going through her shit the next day to see if I could find any clues as to who her accomplice was.

"We are not having sex in this house shawty," I finally said.

I watched Schina look around with a slight frown on her face. "Nah, we absolutely aren't. I don't know why if you gonna cheat it can't be with a clean bitch, but whatever. C'mon we can go home for tonight. But tomorrow we gonna come back and tear this mothafucka up until we figure out who the fuck has my kids. At least we know that whoever has them is feeding them. I read that grocery list that was sent to her phone and, yea, that's definitely a Fat Meat list," she said calling Liv by her family nickname.

After I grabbed a few things, we jumped in her Dodge, leaving the Tahoe parked at the house, and we headed home. Just pulling in the driveway made me go through so many emotions, anger, remorse, confusion, and anger all over again. But I just ignored them as I followed her up to the big red door she just had to have after we purchased what was supposed to be our forever home.

As Schina unlocked the door, I heard a car pulling up behind us. I instantly reached for the pistol in my waistband, spinning around ready to fire on any intruders.

I took note of the fact that it was the Camaro that Nicole drove on her off time. I started to place my pistol back in my waistband until I noticed the silhouette behind the tint was entirely too damn big to be Nicole.

Misty Holt

Chapter Fourteen
Ivory

I had been calling Blacc's phone on and off all day with no answer. I was just about to lay it down and say fuck that nigga, even though I was really trying to fuck. But before I could do any of that, I heard Nicki Minaj's *Best Friend* blare from my phone, and I knew Schina was calling.

I immediately was on edge. The last time I had talked to her, she was on the way to that hoe ass nigga Money's house. I knew the hoe was horny, but I didn't understand why she couldn't just use her fucking vibrator. Why would she jump back in the bed with that nigga? Especially considering we had just killed another bitch that his sorry ass had been fucking. But at the end of the day, it was her decision and, even if I didn't agree with it, I had her back at all costs.

"What, hoe? Damn, was it that bad?" I asked her. When she didn't cuss me out immediately, I knew something else was up. I could only sigh and sit back on my black leather couch. I was exhausted. So much shit had gone down in the last couple of months, I wasn't sure how much more I could take. "Just spit it the fuck out, Schina. Fuck."

"Nicole's dead." I had to have heard that shit wrong. I mean, no, she wasn't my favorite person in the world. I had honestly been waiting on her to fuck up so I could fuck her up, but that was between us. Who the fuck would have the audacity to bring not just harm, but death to a mothafucking Queen? I didn't have the answers to those questions yet, and I wasn't sure if Schina did either, but I knew between the fact that my godchildren were still missing and the third of our terrible trio was dead, I knew Dallas was again about to lay the fuck down.

"Ivory. Ivory? Are you there, bestie," as I tuned back into the phone call I couldn't believe I was having, I heard the tears and anger in her voice. I knew then I had to accept that this was a reality.

"Yea, I'm here. What hospital are y'all at? How come you're just now calling me?" My question was followed by a pause that I wasn't feeling. "Schina, god damn. Quit playing and tell me what the fuck is going on."

"Well, her body is at Parkland, but I'm at my house with Money and…"

Assuming that she was going to say the cops were still there and that was who had made the notification, I quickly slid my feet into my house shoes. I grabbed my keys and disconnected the call. I wasn't feeling all the mysteriousness behind her call and I needed to be able to look her in the eyes as she explained to me what the fuck was going on.

I lived on the far side of North Dallas, and it usually took me at least thirty minutes to get to her house in Rowlett. Considering it was late night, traffic was sparse and I was determined to get my ass over there, that night it took only twenty. I immediately became confused as I saw Nicole's Camaro sitting in the driveway. I grabbed my keys and ran to the front door. I bypassed using my key and instead began beating on the door like a madman.

The door was snatched open and Schina launched herself into my arms. "I can't believe this, Ivory. And I was so mean to her today."

I pulled back from her so I could look her in her eyes. "Nah, you weren't mean to her, and trust me, she knew you meant well. But I need to know what the fuck is going on. How did her car get here? How did you find out?"

"I told her." I just knew my ears had to be playing tricks on me. I stared into my best friends eyes, hoping she would tell me that I was just tripping, but her eyes just showed sympathy.

I was even more confused. "Wait a minute. I need someone to make me understand what the fuck is going on." I had completely forgotten where I was and I had begun yelling. I noticed porch lights coming on all around us and knew I needed to go in the house before I really started acting an ass. "You know what, don't answer a fucking question. I have a feeling I'm going to need to at least try to get high for this shit."

I went back to my truck and grabbed my purse and my glock out of the glove box. All I knew was this nigga had better say some good shit, or he was going to be visiting Nicole a lot sooner than he intended to.

Once I was in the house and seated on the couch, I started breaking down some weed and staring at everyone like they were strangers. "Okay, someone say something." I heard Blacc as he cleared his throat and shot a glance at Schina, like she could help him. "Nah, nigga, don't be looking for her fucking help. I know where her ass been. Ah hell, I guess I know where yo punk ass been, too, huh? But I don't know why yo black ass standing there and my girl is dead, so start fucking talking before that's not the case."

"Where would you like me to start," he asked in that macho voice that used to send me over the edge.

"I want you to start at the mothafucking beginning. At whatever part had you with my girl when she died. At whatever part made you comfortable enough to get yo mulatto ass in my friend's car and drive yo self to Rowlett to tell my sister she's dead. How about starting there, nigga." I was beyond pissed and I made sure that my words conveyed that shit. Fuck him and his feelings.

"Well, Nicole and I have been talking for the last couple of weeks." I had to jerk my head back up.

"Nigga, a couple of weeks? You ain't been out but for a couple of weeks."

"Yea, and you know yo ass been busy. You ain't had no time for a nigga. Hell, you had Nicole pick me up from the Lew. What the fuck did you expect to happen, Ivory?" My ears had to be deceiving me. This had to be some kind of damn dream. I wish this hoe was alive so I could whoop her ass.

"Well, I expected my fellow fucking Queen to have more loyalty than that, but I been telling Schina that hoe wasn't worth shit. I guess I knew better than to expect a damn thing from a nigga, though." I knew I shouldn't be disrespecting Nicole like that and she was freshly dead, but that dead ass hoe was trifling.

"You knew I had been on lock for months and you barely had time for me. I ain't got no ass from you but one time since I've been home. Hell, if I wanted to keep beating my meat I could have stayed in the fucking county." He said that shit so seriously it took all I had not to put a bullet in his ass. Reading my mind the way that we do, Schina reached out and grabbed my pistol from the table and handed it to that dog that she was married to.

"Yea, nigga, I knew yo ass had been on lock, but on the same token, you knew that my god children have been missing for almost a god damn month. Man, what a bitch got to do to get some loyalty around this bitch?" That's when it struck me how calm my very own best friend was being about this situation. I jerked my head in her direction. "Bitch, please tell me you ain't know about this fuckery."

I heard her suck her teeth as she stared at me in contempt. "You know what, I'ma let that shit slide, hoe, cuz I know you feeling some kind of way. But you know damn well how my loyalty is set up."

She was right and I knew I would need to apologize to her later, but right then wasn't going to be the time. "You know what, nigga, I don't even want to hear no more about y'all's personal shit. Just tell me how her ass died and who the fuck did it so we can go handle that shit and I can get the fuck out yo presence." I was mad as hell, but she was still one of us and no one got a pass for taking out one of the crew. Ever.

I watched as he ran his hand across his face and took a deep breath. "So today was the day to count up, so she could deliver the money to my dad and get ready for the next pick up. We did the count and it turns out that the niggas over there on Bexar Street were 5 g's short."

"Wait a minute," I was sure Schina was about to ask the same damn question that immediately went through my mind. "Why the hell would she accept the money from them without counting it right then and there? That's just inviting a nigga to try their hand."

"Yea, and I kept telling her ass that, but she wasn't listening. She had this system where each hood had drop bags with certain pictures on them so she could know who dropped what, and she relied on that shit. Up until yesterday, no one had tried her." He was shaking his head the whole time he was telling us. Had he fallen in love with my own friend? At this point, did it even matter? *Probably not,* I answered myself.

"Okay, so after y'all figured out who was short, what happened?" I looked at Money like he had grown two heads. Since when did crew shit matter to him? "Don't start no shit, Ivory. We have bigger issues right now than your problems with me."

"Whatever, Byron," I responded, while motioning with my hand for Blacc to continue with his story.

"Well, she called up Tye and James and we rode out to check them niggas, but it was a setup. It had to have been, because she didn't even call them niggas and ask about the money, we just rolled out." I watched him get a faraway look in his eyes and I could tell that he was replaying the whole scene over in his head.

"Nigga, we don't have time for all that, just tell me what the fuck happened to my sister." Even Schina was getting impatient with the story and that was never a good thing.

"My bad, y'all. It was just so crazy. We pulled up to the blue house on Bexar and we all unloaded from the truck. She was about to use her key to let us all in the house, but the door swung open. Standing there was this lil chic and about five other niggas. They were all strapped heavy, my nigga, and the bitch was crying hysterically. Shawty must have recognized her because she immediately pointed her strap at ole girl's face." It was then that I heard the emotion in his voice. Even though he was feeling it about my friend, I still wanted to comfort him. I scooted closer to him on the couch and put my arm around him.

"It's all good, Blacc. I'm sure by now you know how the crew gets down and retaliation is a way of life around these parts," I tried to reassure him. "What did ole' girl look like, though?"

"Man, I don't even know. That shit happened so fast. Ole girl said something about y'all had taken too many people from her and that shit was ending today."

Chapter Fifteen
Schina

Before Blacc could finish his story, I received a text. I was going to ignore it but it was followed by two more, so I snatched it off the coffee table and glared at the screen. I was more than ready to go the hell off on whoever it was. That was until I saw that all three messages were one word messages. 'Mama.'

"It's one of the girls." Shit was happening too damn fast for me. Could all of this shit be tied into each other? I wasn't sure but I was damn sure about to find out. "We need to call Ni... Fuck."

I did something I tried to never do. I broke down to my knees in sobs. As I cried all of my fears, sorrow, and anger into my hands, I felt two strong hands pull me to my feet. I could tell by the scent that it was my baby, and I definitely needed his strength at the moment.

"It's all good, shawty. Let it out, but know that we are going to fix everything. We gonna find our girls and we gonna get them Bexar Street niggas. Don't forget we did background checks on all them niggas. If we have to, we will slay their whole families, starting with their mothers. Now get your cries out, baby, but we gotta boss up. We need to call a meeting with all the captains. We need to get better organized. We need a crew mainly for getting them niggas and then we need a crew for looking for the girls. That's one problem. Y'all been trying to do everything without using the resources you have. It's time to boss up, babe."

I knew he was right, and listening to him give me a speech I was sure I had given him before made me dry my tears real quick. "Yea, you're right. But before I do a damn thing, I'm about to text my daughter back." I grabbed my phone and replied to the message. "Where are you so I can come get you?" There was nothing more important.

While I waited for my baby to answer me, I also sent out a mass text to all of the captains from Oak Cliff, West Dallas, East Dallas, Garland, Mesquite, and the North. I wasn't trusting no other mothafucka from the south right now. Too much betrayal had been exposed over there in the last 24 hours and I wasn't feeling that shit.

"I want the whole south shut the fuck down. We can find some new young niggas to run the south." As usual, me and the bestie were on the same wave patterns. That's why she was my ace, I didn't have to say shit, she just knew off top what the hell I would want.

"Yea, I was just thinking the same thing. I just sent out a message for all the captains from every other hood to meet us on Regal Row in an hour, so bring y'all's asses on. Blacc, on the way over, I need you to call your dad and let him know what is going on." I was barking out orders as I put my shoes back on.

"We can all ride in the truck," Ivory said as she started leading the way out the door. I started out behind them, but stopped and ran back to my bedroom first. As much as I loved Bonnie n Clyde, my .50 calibers, I wanted my babies, my .9mms, for whatever was going down tonight.

Just as I locked the door, my phone started going off. This was the first time I truly hated that I had only been carrying one phone. I couldn't tell if this was one of my babies texting me, or someone from the crew. As I ran to the truck I glanced at my screen and saw it was indeed one of my children. "I don't know where we are, mama, but Ms. Ma'am was here and then earlier she left. She was crying and she hasn't been back. She locked us in the bathroom and I can't get the door open. And when she left, she said if her wife was dead we would die, too. We are scared, mama. I can't get Liv to stop crying."

I jumped in the truck but waved at Ivory letting her know not to pull off yet. "How are you texting me, Beautay?" I was wracking my brain trying to figure out who I had crossed that was gay. I knew it couldn't have had anything to do with V because she had been dead.

I reached over and grabbed the cigarette from Ivory's hand. I knew she was about to fuss because of the baby, but I silenced her with a simple look. Not only was I not trying to hear that shit right then, I still hadn't told my husband that I was pregnant. As I waited for the ding of my text message alerts, I let everyone in the truck know what was going on. I also had Money to text Skeet, Funky, Chase, and Chance and tell them to bypass the meeting and come straight to my house.

"Money, you're going to have to man up. I need you to go run that meeting for me. I need you to make sure y'all go find them south Dallas niggas and if you can't, do exactly as you said. I want every single one of them to be mourning their mama tomorrow. If they have children, kill their baby mamas, too. It's time we remind the streets exactly who the fuck we are. This ain't no fucking game. I'm taking my lil crew and going to get my fucking kids. Now, nigga, go."

He reached across the seat and kissed me on my cheek. "I got you, shawty. I won't let you down. Too much of this has been behind my bullshit and it's time I make it up to you as much as possible. Do you want me to take Blacc with me?"

I had to stop and think about that. As much as I wanted to trust Blacc, I already saw that he could be a trifling ass dude. But then I thought of the love that his dad had for me.

"Yea, go on and take him. I have no doubt that if he betrays the crew, Jorge will have his head."

Just as they slammed their doors and headed towards Nicole's Camaro, my phone dinged. "We have tablets, mama." I thought carefully on how the fact that they had tablets could help me find their location. I felt Ivory looking at my screen as well and knew she was doing the same thing. I was just about to scream out in frustration when it hit me. GPS.

"Okay, baby. I need you to go into the main menu and find the maps. Once you open it, I need you to put in our address as the final destination. When you do that, I need you to tell me exactly what it says the starting point is okay."

This time the response was almost immediate and in my mind I could picture my babies huddled up in a bathroom trying to comfort each other. "Okay, mama." It was a few minutes before she sent me an address but I knew exactly where it was.

"Bitch, you know those apartments off of Munger," I asked as I looked Ivory right in her eyes. She didn't even say a word, just nodded her head and pulled out, turning the truck in the direction that we were headed in.

"Okay, baby, I know where you are. But I don't know what apartment it is. I need you to give me some kind of clue my love." I could only hope that she had seen a door number or something that would lead me to the apartment that they were holed up in.

"I don't know, mama. She put something over our heads when we got here, but I know that we are upstairs. And sometimes I can hear the people downstairs playing loud Mexico music." Well that didn't help much, but I would run my ass up in every apartment on the second floor of the whole damn complex if that's what the fuck it took. Now that I was this close to having my babies back home with me, not a damn thing was going to step in my way.

"Okay, baby. I'm on my way and I'm going to find you, my love. By the end of the night you will be in your own room watching YouTube videos on your own TV. I love you, baby."

"I love you too, mama. Liv says please hurry, she really misses you."

I didn't even respond, I just laid my head back on the head-rest. "Bitch, you gone have to drive faster than this. I need to get to my motherfucking kids." Ivory also didn't verbally respond. She let the jumping of the truck's engine speak for her.

What seemed to me to be an eternity later, but according to my baby's last message was in reality only fifteen minutes, we were reaching our destination. Just as Ivory parked the truck in the back of the complex as we had discussed on the way over, a brilliant idea came to me. I pulled my phone back out and I sent a text to my baby girl. "Are y'all still alone in the bathroom?"

"Yes, mama."

"Okay, baby, I need y'all to start banging around. Tear up shit. Scream. I need y'all to make as much noise as possible. Start now, okay, Tai?"

"Ok, mama," was the short reply.

I turned and looked at Ivory and told her what my idea was. "Yea, that makes sense. Well you start at that end of the side-walk," she said pointing to the left. "And I'll start down there."

We split up and headed in our opposite directions, both of us with our pistols down by our side. I had never listened for any noise as intently as I was at that moment. Nothing else was as important as having my children home. I knew Ivory would be glad when we got them home, too. She had refused to bring her own daughter home until we not only had the girls home, but knew who had taken them as well.

One thing that was going to make this easier was that there were only four apartments per building. There were two upstairs and two downstairs. Having breeze-ways probably would have made it a more difficult task, not that it would have mattered to me. As I headed to the first set of steps, I had this eerie feeling that someone was watching me. I didn't slow my steps but I did let my head swivel, trying to stay alert to my surroundings.

I didn't want to put any of the innocent people in the complex in danger, but I would turn this bitch into a scene from Vietnam if I had to. I had barely made it to the top of the stairs when I saw a vaguely familiar woman rushing into the next set. I also thought I heard some banging coming from that direction. I did stop, then. I craned my neck in that direction wondering if I was tripping.

I ran down the steps and headed in the direction doing three things simultaneously. I pulled my pistols, shouted for Ivory, and remembered that I never texted Funky and told him where we were headed. "Fuck," I said out loud as I headed in the direction I had seen ol' girl run in.

Chapter Sixteen
S

I have to be tripping, I thought to myself as I saw someone start to climb the stairs in the unit next to mine. I rubbed my eyes and stared at her again. Nah, I wasn't tripping. That really was Schina. I didn't know how the hell she had found me, but I wasn't giving up her little bastards without a fight. That bitch and her nigga had taken too damn much from me and it was past my time to get even.

I got out of my car and tried my best to be as inconspicuous as possible as I headed towards my second floor apartment. As I neared the stairs, I saw Schina's head snap in my direction. I didn't change my pace as she had only seen me once before, and my appearance had been quite different.

As I began lightly jogging up the stairs, I noticed an almost rhythmic banging. I knew it had to be the children, and I figured that was their way of helping their mother figure out what apartment they were in. *Too bad I'm going to reach them first*, I thought as I broke into an outright run.

I could hear feet pounding the pavement behind me as I reached my front door. I hurried and stuck my key in the door and pushed the door open, peeking behind me to see their mom taking the steps two at a time.

"Bitch, you better not harm a hair on my motherfucking..." Her words were cut off as I slammed the door and locked it behind me. Fuck her and her fucking kids. I had no doubt she would get through my flimsy ass door after a kick or two, but I would have at least one of her precious babies in my hands before that happened. To make sure I was right, I ran to the bathroom door and hurriedly shoved the couch I had barricaded the door with. I needed in that bathroom as soon as possible. I was so determined to make it happen I had completely tuned out all of that damn noise they were making.

Boom. I heard the first kick at my door just as I entered the bathroom. I quickly snatched the first kid I could reach and pulled her out of the bathroom. "Oh, y'all wanna play games, huh? Well someone's going to die today," I said to who I now noticed was the youngest child. I started dragging her to the kitchen and grabbed the largest knife in my butcher's block, just as my front door caved in.

"Bitch, where are my kids?" Her voice seemed to sound like it had come from some form of mythical monster.

"Well, hello there," I replied more calmly than I was actually feeling. "Seems like we are about to have one of those standoffs you read about in those street lit books."

The bitch had the audacity to laugh, like I wasn't holding a knife to her damn kid's neck. "Bitch, I promise if you hurt my baby, I will slaughter everyone you have ever loved."

"You can't be serious. There's no one else for you to go after. Y'all have taken both of my brothers, I can only stand for small periods of time, and now the woman I planned on spending the rest of my life with is gone as well. What the fuck else can you take from me?" If she only knew how serious I was. Bam was the only person I had left. The only person I still had to love, and now she was gone, too. I had nothing else to lose. Death wasn't even a fear of mine, anymore.

"I don't know you or your bitch ass brothers, but unless you want to go visit those niggas, you should release my daughter." She was talking hot shit and I had to let her know I was dead ass serious, so I pricked Thing Two with the knife. Not hard enough to kill her, because I wasn't through with the game, but hard enough to cause her to scream and to cause a small steady stream of blood to flow from her neck.

"You really should think harder about the consequences of your actions," I spat. "Now this is what's going to happen. Throw your gun over here." She did that and I continued with my directions. "Now, I know you aren't alone, so you're going to stick your head out the door and tell that fat bitch that follows you everywhere to tear her monkey ass. And do it now." She seemed to hesitate but then I saw her glance in her daughter's eyes. I guess the reality of what was taking place hit her because her shoulders slumped and she did as I asked.

"Okay, that's done. Why don't you tell me who the hell you are and what is it that you want." I couldn't believe she was still issuing out demands, but I had always heard she wasn't good at taking directions.

"You don't get to make demands right now. I'm the one…" I was just about to put my foot down when I felt this piercing pain in my side. I looked down and Thing One had just stuck me in my side with a much smaller knife than the one I was holding to her sister's neck. Out of reflex, I reached out and slapped the hell out of her. I watched in almost slow motion as she went falling backwards and bashed her head on the kitchen counter.

"Noooo," her mama yelled as she slid to the ground and laid motionless. "What did you do to my baby? Tai, please get up, baby. Please get up and come to mama." Tears were streaming down her face and even though I couldn't see Thing two's face, I knew she, too, was crying. I could tell because I could feel the warmth of the tears as they hit the arm that I had snaked around her neck.

"Well, bitch, I guess you better cooperate while you still have one, huh?" Even though I had grown fond of the children in the time that I'd held them captive, I no longer gave a fuck about them. When I realized that Bam was gone, my heart had completely frozen over. No one mattered anymore.

"Please, just let my babies go. You can take me in their place. They are innocent. They haven't done anything to you." There it was, the begging and sniveling that I thought I wanted so damn bad. I just didn't understand why it wasn't making me feel any better.

"Did Bam beg for her life like that? Hmmm? What about my brother, Shawn?" I watched as confusion shot across her face.

"I don't even know anyone named Shawn," she muttered with her eyes glued to her daughter who was still slumped on the floor.

"Bitch, you kill so many people that you can't even remember all of them?" I saw the guilt wash across her face and instantly had my answer. I shook my head as I tried to decide how I really wanted to play this shit out. "Look, this what I want you to do. I want you to walk over to that couch right there and have a seat. We gone talk about the transgressions you have made against my family and then I will decide on who, if any of you, are going to walk up outta here."

She didn't know it, but I needed her to sit down so I could have a seat, too. I figured if she sat on the couch I could sit at the dining room table with the kid on the floor at my feet. That way I could still hold the knife to her neck. I would also still be able to see the front door. There was no doubt in my mind that more people would be showing up soon. I was okay with that. I just hoped that bitch nigga Money was one of the cavalry who showed up to save the day.

She did as I asked, still sobbing and shifting her eyes between her two daughters. I flashed back to my parents and I couldn't help but to wish that they loved me as much as she seemed to love her kids, but it was too late to go back to those days.

"Now that I'm sitting, can you explain to me who Shawn is? And you keep saying I took someone else from you? Who?" She asked all of this as I shuffle stepped me and her youngest to the dining room chair. Even though it was just a few steps away, to me that seemed to be a whole football field.

"Yea, hoe, I'ma tell you." I let my emotions get to me and I squeezed on the kid's neck enough to emit a squeal from her, causing everyone in the room to jump. Well, everyone except her older sister who was still slumped over. I was actually beginning to wonder if I had killed her. "My bad, child, just hold still as I tell ya mama a lil story."

"Yes, Ms. Ma'am. Please just don't hurt me or my mama like you hurt my sister." The pleading sound in her voice almost made me feel bad. Almost but not quite. Obviously, her mama ain't feel bad when she put them slugs in my brother's head. Hell, she couldn't even remember who the hell he was.

"If ya mama sit there and do what the hell I tell her to do, you and your sister might walk up out of here. Now, Schina, I want you to think back. Think back to one day you're at the mall and you just met the man who you now call ya husband." I watched the recognition cross her face and I knew she now knew who the hell I was.

"Shawnta, but I thought you were…" Her words trailed off as she gestured at my legs with her hands.

"You thought I was paralyzed? Yea, I was. For many years after that hoe ass nigga beat my ass, I was completely unable to use my legs. But my brother, Steffon, had me in therapy all this time. Now, I can walk and stand, for short amounts of time. Speaking of Steffon, I know Money had him killed, too. Now do you understand why you are going through the shit you are going through, hoe," I said, letting emotions cause me to stick the child in the other side of her neck. This time Schina didn't cry, I watched pure anger cross her face.

"Let me tell you something, Shawnta. First off, that day at the mall, I had no idea that was your brother. As a matter of fact, I had no idea what the hell was going on. All I knew was I had a one year old daughter at home." With the mention of her daughter, her eyes shot back over to her oldest. "I was determined to make it to my baby. There was no way in hell I was about to let some random ass person run me over in the mall parking lot. I'm sorry that you lost a brother that day, I am. But I couldn't just let my daughter grow up with no mother." One thing I had to say, she stood by her beliefs regardless of what situation she found herself in, and while I could respect it, it didn't alleviate my pain any.

Chapter Seventeen
Money

It took twenty minutes from when Ivory called and let me know what was going on for me to pull up in the parking lot she told me she was sitting in. I had spent the entire twenty minutes trying to figure out who the hell it could have been. I was jumping out of the car and I still had no idea who the hell we were going against.

So much shit was going on, it was like my head was spinning. I grabbed my pistol and stuck it in my waistband as I strutted over to where Ivory was sitting on the bottom step of a staircase in the middle of the back parking lot.

"Ivory, tell me something." I could hear the pleading tone in my voice and at that moment I didn't even care. I just wanted my family to be okay and safe. Even if we never worked things out, Schina and those girls were my life. It always took some drastic ass situation for me to realize how much I loved and needed them, but it was what it was.

"Well, I sat and listened for a while. Ol' girl said something about Bam was the love of her life and Schina took her brother Shawn from her." Shawnta? It couldn't be. I didn't give Ivory a chance to say another word, before I started sprinting up the stairs.

"Wait right here. The crew should be just a few minutes behind me. Fill them in. Let Blue know I think it's Shawnta ass."

"Shawnta?" I heard the confusion in her voice as I kept heading up the stairs. I knew what she wanted to ask, but I simply didn't have time to answer any questions. That bitch had always been unstable as fuck, and I had to try to get my family out of this situation. I couldn't lose one of my children, or my wife, behind this dumb ass shit. We had all been through enough. Hell, Schina hadn't even had time to mourn Nicole properly.

I skidded to a stop at the top of the stairs and noticed that the door was kicked in, so entering the apartment wouldn't be an issue. But I knew before I went galloping in like a knight in shining armor, I needed to hear what was going on.

I heard my wife's voice and it sounded like she was trying to convince Shawnta that she hadn't meant to take her brother's life. And she hadn't. She was simply trying to save mine. There we were again, and my dick had us in some shit. Even if me and Schina never worked out, I had to start being more careful about who I slang the D to.

I sat and listened to them for a while before I poked my head around the corner. I was hoping that no one saw me, and for once luck was on my side. Shawnta was so focused on Schina and trying to place the blame on her shoulders, she was paying no attention to the open door.

Well, that's what I thought until I heard her say, "Aah, look who's here. Come on in, Money. Now we can really get this party started." Fuck. I was really trying to go in on some surprise type shit, but since I couldn't, there was nothing to do but go in. Maybe I could talk our way out of this situation. I had always had a gift of gab, and I could only hope it didn't fail me.

"Shawnta, why are you doing this?" I really knew why she was doing it, but I needed to stall. While I still had my pistols in my waist, she still had a knife to my baby girl's neck. I didn't have any doubt that she would kill her by the time I pulled out and finger fucked the trigger.

"Nigga, don't play. You know why the fuck I'm doing this. Now go have a seat over there by your precious ass wife, while I decide on what the fuck I want to happen from here."

As I walked over to the dingy ass couch Schina was sitting on, I thought I saw Tai twitch. I didn't look over to see if I was right. I did take notice that there was only one of Schina's pink pistols on the ground. That meant two things to me. It meant that

Schina had at least one pistol and it also meant that Tai may be the one to save us.

Against my better judgement, Schina had been taking that girl to the gun range since she was six years old. She damn near had a better shot than me, and it looked like it may finally pay off. As I sat down next to Schina, I made the slightest nod of my head towards Tai. I knew she would catch it, Schina noticed everything. She was very in tune with the people around her at all times. As I saw Schina also notice that Tai was making the slightest movements, I tried to think of a way to help us all out.

"Money, please tell her I had no idea who was in that truck that day at the mall," Schina almost pleaded. I wondered why she would ask that of all things. I knew they had already discussed that situation and it didn't seem like she gave a damn about us not knowing who was in the truck. I shot her a confused look and that's when I saw the slight hand movements that she was making.

Sign language. She was telling Tai what she needed her to do. Understanding what the hell was going on, I did exactly what she needed me to do, continued to distract the one with the knife. "Shawnta, you know she's right. We had just met that day. There's no way we had planned to kill Shawn that day. We were just about to leave the mall and go have lunch when he tried to run us over," I explained, using lots of hand gestures. I wanted to make sure that she kept her focus on me.

"Fuck what you're talking about. And y'all must think I'm stupid as fuck." Thinking that she had caught on to what we were trying to do, my stomach dropped to my feet. I glanced at Schina and her face had gone white. The fear for our children was written all in her eyes.

"What are you talking about," shawty asked. I hated hearing the tremble in her voice. Usually, nothing could scare her. It just wasn't an emotion that she felt. Anger, sadness, happiness, yes. But never had I known her to be scared.

"I know your bitch ass husband has a gun and I need him to slide that shit over here." *Whew*, I thought. The sense of relief that washed over my body was immediate and almost over-whelming. So much so, I didn't even protest as I pulled one of the pistols from my waistband and slid it across the floor with no complaints. "There, now that's much better." I watched as she dropped the knife she was holding and reached down and grabbed my strap. The only good thing about that was she was just holding it loosely and wasn't pointing it at my baby's head, or anything in particular. She was definitely a novice at the hos-tage holding thing. She should have called Schina and got some tips.

Trying to keep her talking, I asked a question I knew would probably lead to a lengthy and long-winded answer. "So I guess I do know why you're doing this. But what else have you been behind?" I figured I could kill two birds with one stone with that question. A lot of shit had been going down over the last couple of months. If I knew what to charge to her, I would know what issues needed to be addressed when and if we got the hell up out of that apartment.

I heard Shawnta laugh one of the most evil laughs I had ever heard. "Oh, you wanna know what else I've done to your lil posse, huh?" She was so pleased with herself she almost let go of Liv's neck. Almost, but not quite. "Let's see, there was the video you received. You know the one. The one that almost got your precious and not so fucking pure wife killed. I was hoping you would beat her ass the way you beat mine."

"*You* sent that shit?" Schina was so pissed, she jumped up from the couch. She was about to lunge for her, until she looked down the barrel of my pistol.

"I'd sit your thot ass down, if I was you, hoe." I saw all the air deflate from wifey's body as she collapsed back down to the couch. She wasn't used to being the one taking orders, especially not at gun point, and it was really starting to get to her, I could tell. I just wondered if Shawnta could, too. "Hell yea, I sent that shit. I was hoping he would beat your bitch ass down the same way he did mine. Why the fuck I have to be in a damn wheelchair for years and your ass got to walk around like you were so fucking perfect? And just as I started to get better, the person who was paying for my therapy mysteriously comes up dead, too. Fuck you, hoe. Too bad he let your ass fucking live."

"I just have one question. How the hell did you get the damn video?" I hadn't even thought of that. I guess if I had to be held captive, I was glad I was with Schina.

Shawnta spat out that evil ass laugh again. "I had been fucking D.B. for years. I knew everything that he had planned out against you. I know you didn't think that dumb ass nigga was smart enough to plan all that shit out by his damn self."

"That fucking figures. All the fucking psychopaths in Dallas just teamed up and decided to gang up on my ass," Schina mumbled under her breath. I did notice her hands were moving again. I also noticed Tai's head was riveted in her direction and her eyes were open. If you weren't her parent you probably wouldn't catch it, though. At least that's what I was hoping.

"What you say, hoe? You know what it don't even matter. I've decided you won't leave this fucking apartment alive."

"Wait, wait, wait," I intervened. "Didn't you send a message that said you wanted money and you would let the girls go?"

I saw a look of pain cross her face before she gave me a reply. "Yea, that was the plan. But see, y'all changed everything when y'all killed my baby. If y'all would have just let Bam go, then maybe I would have followed through with the initial plan, but y'all took the last person I had. Someone is going to die in this bitch today. And I'll be honest, at first I was planning on it being you, Byron. I mean, after all, you are the common denominator." I felt wifey's head snap in my direction. I also felt the lasers I was sure she was shooting at me with her eyes. "Yea, his hoe ways keep you in some shit, huh? But yea, I was going to kill you, but then I realized if I kill you, this hoe, y'all's so called crew, and even these damn kids would be able to go on. Probably like hadn't shit happened. I mean, everyone all over Dallas knows that it's her and her girls that keep y'all's shit together, right? Oh, wait, y'all are short one bitch now, aren't y'all?" she chuckled as she directed that question at Schina, who was now sitting board straight next to me.

"You mean to tell me you were the bitch at the house on Bexar Street," Schina asked in between teeth that were clinched tight. I could almost hear them cracking.

"Yep, I did that shit…" And that's when all hell broke loose. I saw Tai grab the gun from the floor and point it at Shawnta's head. At the same time, I saw Shawnta point the gun she had retrieved from the floor at Schina's head.

"No, Tai. Waiiiii…" I yelled. But it was too late. *Boom, Boom*, was all I heard as I turned to my wife.

Chapter Eighteen
Schina

"This hoe better not have shot my baby," I yelled as I pulled the pistol she hadn't asked about out of my waistband. I didn't even take a second to think about what was going on as I pointed my gun at that hoe's leaning body. I emptied my whole damn clip. I was going to make sure that bitch caused no more chaos in my life before I did another motherfucking thing. Once I had reassured myself that her days of drama were over, I looked around the room. Money. Check. Tai. Check. "Oh my god. Where is my baby?"

I noticed out of the corner of my eye that Ivory and the cavalry were now running into the apartment. It didn't even matter anymore. Where the fuck were they when I needed them? I let my eyes scan the room until I found Money squatting over Liv, whose eyes were wide open. "Mama, I missed you."

Those were the sweetest words I had ever heard. Since I knew my baby was okay, I ran over to Tai and hugged her.

"Baby, you did a great job. You just saved all of our lives," I cried as I pulled her into my arms. That's when I noticed her body was shaking uncontrollably. I hadn't taken into consideration my children were just thrust into a world I had done everything to shield them from. There would definitely be emotional repercussions for a very long time.

"Mama, I was so scared. But I read your hands when you told me I was the only one who could save us. I read your hands when you told me to grab your gun." She was crying into my shoulder by that point. I just wanted to make my baby girl feel better.

"Y'all call the cleanup crew. There's too many signs of my children and us having been here," I spat directions at Ivory and the men that were behind her. "Money, grab Liv, let's go home. Our babies need to go home to their own house."

I grabbed Tai's hand and led her through what I'm sure to them felt like a prison cell. We descended the stairs two by two and I realized how normal the sounds of gunfire must be in that neighborhood. I didn't see one nosy ass neighbor that would have to be dealt with. That was something I was grateful for.

For the first time since we had entered the dope game, I was tired of death and carnage. Maybe it was because I had lost one of my best friends. But most likely, it was because I was on the verge of feeling the mourning, grief, and anger that I had made so many other mothers feel. Whatever it was, it made me open my eyes to a lot of things.

As we climbed into Ivory's truck, that just happened to still have the keys in the ignition, I looked at Money. "Boo, I think I'm ready to get out of this street life. It's time for me to slow my ass down and be a mother. I'm tired, boo."

I turned back and looked at my daughters, both of whom were crying, but not as hysterically. Yea, it was time for me to give up the street life. I had almost lost my kids behind some bullshit.

"What about the drop that was just made? What you gonna tell Jorge?" I had to weigh the tone of his words before I answered. I needed to know if he was asking for selfish reasons or was he really concerned.

"Well, you, Ivory, and Blue can handle it. Jorge won't trip as long as business is handled. Before all the bullshit, you and I had talked about you taking your rightful place as the head of this family. This just proves that we were right. If I had been at home with my babies, none of this shit would have happened. As much as I love the streets, I love the girls more." I became emotional as I was talking. I was glad that I was letting Money drive. I probably would have driven us right off the 35 bridge, I was crying so hard.

"Mama, it's not your fault. We know that you do whatever you do to make sure that we have all the things we want." My baby, Liv, had finally started talking, and I was so happy for that. I just knew she was going to be mad traumatized and it was going to take forever to get her to speak. But nope, there she was trying to comfort me when I should be the one trying to comfort her. If I believed in a God, I would be thanking him for giving me such strong kids.

"No, Liv, it's never okay for parents to let harm come to their children. While I may succeed in giving you the material things you deserve, I failed at giving you the most important things. I haven't given you safety or stability, and I promise that all that is about to change. From here on out, it's us against the world, ladies." It was then that I realized, hell, they should have been in school two weeks ago. I had no way to explain to the district, without getting them all involved in my business, why the girls hadn't been in school. Considering it was Friday, I had two days to try to come up with something.

***

"Mama, can you make me some chicken?" Liv had just got out of the shower, and while I was expecting her to be withdrawn and scared of everything, for the moment, she was my sweet greedy little baby.

"Of course I can. Let's see what Tai wants for dinner and we can run to Albertson's and get whatever we need. Maybe she will even want to go with us," I said in response to her question.

"You know she don't wanna go," Liv laughed as she grabbed my hand. She started pulling me to the media room where Money and Tai were watching the Longhorns play Texas A&M.

"Probably not, but it doesn't hurt to ask," I said as we rounded the corner.

As we got closer, I could hear what sounded like crying. I immediately was on edge. "Liv, go back in the living room and wait for me, okay?" I felt her hesitate and I realized that that's where the consequences of everything that had happened was going to lie. My baby was going to be scared to be alone. Even in her own safe place. Realizing that pissed me off and I wished I could kill that bitch all over again. "It's okay, you can come in with me, but I need to talk to Tai, so I need you to sit closer to the door, is that okay, my love?"

"Okay, mama," she said in what was almost a baby voice. I pondered therapy for them as we finally entered the media room.

What I saw before me seemed to freeze and melt my heart all in one instant. Tai had taken a shower and put on some blue Roblox pajamas. Roblox was some game she was highly addicted to. She had pulled her hair back in a ponytail and Money was rubbing her head as she laid her head on his shoulder and cried. Crying was something foreign for Tai. She was the kind of kid, instead of crying, she would just get pissed off about the things that were bothering her, kinda like her mama.

"But am I going to be in trouble, dad? Am I going to go to jail?" The fact that this was something that was bothering my eleven year old was pissing me off even more.

I started to walk over and put my two cents in, but Money raised his head, saw me and waved me off. I mimicked driving and a baby sign to let him know me and Liv were about to leave. I knew he would handle this situation with care, and she would probably take to him better than me, so I just decided I would buy the things for Tai's favorite meal without disturbing them.

I made the shhh signal to Liv and grabbed her hand, pulling her out of the media room behind me. Once we had made it to the living room, Liv slightly tugged at my hand. "Mama, you didn't ask Tai what she wants to eat." She was such a sweet girl, always thinking of others.

"I know, baby. I'm going to get some ribs, corn on the cob, and potato salad for her meal. Don't you think that will be a winner for her?"

Her eyes lit up and she nodded her head. Anyone who knew Tai, knew that was her favorite meal. Since Tai was the only one in the household who ate pork, cooking two meals at one time wasn't anything new. I damn sure wasn't about to complain. I was just happy to have my babies home.

I grabbed my purse, keys, and phone and led Liv out to the front door and to my car. As we headed to the grocery store that was only minutes away from our house, my phone rang.

"Hello," I answered without glancing at the caller ID. I noticed that had become a bad habit lately and I definitely needed to change it. I wasn't in the mood to talk to just anyone.

"Mija, my son says that the girls are home. Is this true?" It was Jorge. It had completely skipped my mind to call him and tell him he could call off his end of the search as well.

"Si, Jorge, I have my babies home. As a matter of fact the youngest and I are on the way to the grocery store."

"That is good, mija. Now that you have gotten that stress off your back, you and I need to talk. We have a problem and it needs to be solved as soon as possible." I knew whatever it was, it had to be weighing on him very heavily because his Mexican accent was more pronounced than usual.

"That is fine, Jorge. I also need to speak to you about some things. Just book a flight for Ivory, Money, me, and the girls," I started to reply to him.

"No, Schina. This time I will be coming to you. I will see you on Monday evening. I will call and let you know where to meet me. I will see you in two days. Adios."

As I parked my car in the parking lot of the grocery store, I wondered what could be so bad that Jorge had to come to the States. I didn't let it bother me for too long, though. I was going to enjoy this weekend with my family. I wasn't even going to let the fact that we were no longer a family take away from this weekend.

***

It was later that night, and we were all snuggled up watching *Secret Life of Pets*. I had just gotten a copy from my bootleg, Slim. My laughter was interrupted by so-called morning sickness. At night. I thought about how stupid it was for them to call it morning sickness when it hit at all times of the day, as I ran to the nearest bathroom.

As I threw up what felt like all of my insides, I heard the door to the bathroom swing open. I was fully expecting it to be Liv. I was almost shocked that it was Money. He always had a weak stomach and managed to make himself scarce whenever someone was sick to their stomach.

"Is there something you need to tell me?"

Chapter Nineteen
Ivory

It had been a long few days and I was all too happy to be home. It seemed like I hadn't had a good night's rest since we left Mexico. Now that Schina was somewhat back to normal, and the girls were home, I was determined to sleep and then sleep some more.

After taking a blunt of loud to the face, I had finally crawled up in my bed. I was reading a Ca$h book, that Schina had recommended, when I was startled by the ringing of my phone. "Ugh, who the fuck is this," I said to no-one. I reached out and grabbed my phone from the nightstand sitting beside my bed. I rolled my eyes towards the ceiling as I noticed the name on the screen. "Ah hell, no." I wasn't answering for that bitch nigga. There wasn't anything he was spitting that I was trying to hear. I was more than happy when the call disconnected. Just as I went to place the phone back in its rightful place, it began to ring again. I pressed the answer button, wishing he could see the attitude I knew was displayed on my face.

"What the fuck do you want, Blacc," I answered, making note that it was one in the damn morning. I couldn't help but to wonder why the fuck he was calling my ass. It had to be clear to him that I had nothing to say to him.

"Ivory, I know I've hurt you," he started but I had to interrupt him real quick.

"Nah, nigga. You give yourself too much damn credit. Nicole hurt me. You just pissed me the fuck off. You simply didn't matter enough to hurt me, my nigga."

"Okay, whatever it is, I know that it was wrong of me to sleep with your friend. I was selfish. I had just got out and…" Did this nigga really think I wanted to hear his lame ass excuses?

"Nigga, I don't really give a fuck why you chose to do it. It's a wrap between you and me. I'm just hoping there's a good god damn reason on why you are calling me. So what is it?"

I listened as he sighed and, because I had sat across from him at visitation more than once, I could even envision the way he held his head as he started to answer. "Well, I been calling Schina, and she isn't answering."

"Psssh. That's my best friend. Mine. While yea, her and Nicole were close, Schina and I have been through the pits of hell together. If you *hurt* me, you *hurt* her, too. So I'm assuming you need to speak to someone of importance. Call Money, hoe. That's who brought you into our circle, ain't it?" I shook my head as I realized what I had just said. "I guess hoes of a feather..."

I giggled as I waited on him to say something. "If you would have let me finish, then you would know I had been calling him, too. I can't get either one of them to answer and I have some information that's gonna be detrimental to the crew. I need to tell someone and I'm willing to help with the solution before I go home to my dad's estate."

I sighed as I wondered if this was important enough to get out of my bed. I had just received my new Tempurpedic mattresses and pillows and it was just like the commercials said. "Stop by McDonalds and get me the biscuit egg and bacon meal with a sprite and a caramel Frappuccino and come on by, dude. But I'm telling you this, if you're wasting my damn time, I'ma shoot you in the left ass cheek, and that's a promise."

"I'll be there in thirty," was all I heard as the call disconnected.

"Damn," I said out loud as I climbed out of my bed. And I literally had to climb. My bed sat so high off the ground I had a custom made purple stool that I normally used to get in and out of the bed. The night before, though, I had kicked it when I climbed in the bed and I was too tired to get down and retrieve it.

Once I climbed out of the bed and let my feet curl into the deep dark grey carpet that covered my bedroom floor, I stretched and walked into my bathroom. Just like my bedroom was decorated in all greys, purples, and whites, so was my bathroom. I emptied my bladder, brushed my teeth, and used a scrunchie to pull my hair back out of my face. I debated on whether I was going to change clothes or not, before I decided fuck it. I simply threw on some black boy shorts that said bossy across the ass. If my white camisole and boy shorts bothered him, too damn bad.

I grabbed my goody bag and walked downstairs to my living room, ready to roll a blunt. I figured by the time I had two blunts rolled he should be pulling up. We could smoke while he told me whatever the fuck was on his mind. Then, hopefully, I could take my ass back to bed. I was fucking tired and seeing his face, knowing he had fucked my friend, was not something that I was looking forward to.

As I sat down on my charcoal grey overstuffed couch, I threw the dark purple throw pillow across the room. "Shit," I said as I almost knocked over the four foot crystal statue of Wonder Woman that Schina had made for my birthday last year. I was tripping throwing anything in my living room, anyway. Everything in here was crystal. I even had a life-size sculpture of me and Schina standing in the corner next to my sixty inch television.

As I rolled the weed, I took a moment to admire my living room. I had only been living in the four bedroom, three bath house since about a month before the trip to Mexico. Due to all the drama, I had barely spent any time in it.

Once you entered the arched doorway, you were facing a huge, dark grey, stone fireplace. Mounted over the fireplace was the television. To the right of that was the statue of me and my bestie. On the other side of that was a loveseat that matched the couch I was seated on. It was also covered with big fat dark purple throw pillows. Laid across the back of the couch was a matching purple chenille throw blanket. Covering the dark grey carpet was a white rug with grey and purple squares all over it. Catty corner to the loveseat was a grey recliner that was big enough to sit three people. I loved to sit there and read. I also had a huge radio in the corner. In the middle of the floor was a huge white marble coffee table that I was using to hold the magazine I had my weed on. The matching end tables sat at the ends of the couch and love seat. My walls were graced with pictures of the Queens, my baby girl Danyelle, and of course my god children. All of the frames were either black or white.

Just as I finished admiring my living room and sealed the last blunt, I heard my doorbell. "Lord, don't let me have to keep my promise and shoot this nigga in his ass cheek." I stared at the heavens as I headed to my huge mahogany front door. I swung the door open and there he was. I had to admit to myself, he was still sexy as fuck. But his chance with me was null and void. "Come on in, nigga. Let's get this shit over with."

I couldn't help but to notice, even though he was the son of a cartel head, he still carried himself and dressed like a straight trap nigga. He had on a black t-shirt with the Jordan silhouette on it, white shorts, and the black and white 12's everyone was just going crazy over. Sitting on top of his head was a black Jordan hat. I swear if my man was the son of a Cartel head, he would dress with some fucking class. That was when I remembered Money had told us that he grew up in the hood. He didn't even know that Jorge was his father until like a year before. Who knew that even men as powerful as Jorge ran off on their responsibilities.

"Do you want this damn food or not?" I guessed he had been holding the bag out to me the whole time I was zoned out. Either way it went, he wasn't about to be raising his voice at me in my own damn house.

"Hold up, bruh. Who is you talking to like that?" I was beyond irritated and I was sure that my voice let him know.

"My bad, Ivory. It's just that I'm stressing and I guess I'm taking that shit out on everyone."

"I hear you, but I'm sure you know my get down well enough to know I ain't that bitch." I snatched the bag of food out of his hand as I led him to the living room. I walked around and had a seat in my recliner and waved him towards the couch.

He looked around before having a seat. "This is a nice place you have, Ivory." He looked at the pictures on the wall and the sculpture in the corner. "You and Schina are very close, huh?"

"Yea, that's my bitch til the end of time. But that's not why you are here, now is it?" I asked as I reached over and grabbed one of the blunts and my purple Bic off the table. I was past ready for him to get to the point and get the fuck out of my house.

He sighed and gave me the side eye as he grabbed the other blunt off the table and held it up. I guessed he was asking permission to light it so I just nodded my head.

"Okay, so I just got wind that someone has been putting counterfeit money in the pickups going out to my dad."

I almost choked on the smoke I had just inhaled. "Nigga, what the fuck are you talking about? That would have to mean Nicole was up to some shady shit and I know you ain't trying to say that, my nigga." I was starting to wish I had grabbed my gun before I let this nigga in. I mean, damn, he was fucking my girl and then he was gone try to put salt on her fucking name, too. Who the fuck did he think he was?

"No, no, no. Just listen," he said, throwing his hands up. "I know who it Is. The problem is, it's one of my dad's so-called men, and I don't know if he's going to believe any of us when we try to tell him."

Okay, that made a little more sense. Nicole might have been a hoe, but she wasn't a thief. She would have no reason to steal. We all made damn good money. Hell, we all owned legitimate businesses that people weren't aware of. "Okay, so I'm assuming you have some kind of damn plan, since you're sitting in my house smoking my weed, so talk, my nigga."

Four blunts and my biscuit sandwich later and I had heard him out. I had to admit it just might work. The only part of the plan I wasn't cool with was not telling Schina until it was all over.

"I don't know, Blacc. That's my best friend and we are basically letting her walk into the lion's den with a steak around her neck."

"Nah, because as soon as it gets heated, you will pull out your phone and let the recording play and everything will be cleared up," he tried to assure me, but I still wasn't understanding why we couldn't just tell her what the hell was going on.

Essentially, Antonio, one of the men Jorge had sent down here to watch over his money, had gotten greedy. He was replacing the real money with fake money and hoping that the crew would take the fall. The only good thing about Blacc fucking with Nicole was he had been by her side bundling and packaging money, so he knew there was no way she had done it. I wasn't exactly sure how he had figured out it was Antonio, but I was just glad that he had.

"Okay, but explain to me again, why we can't tell Schina?"

"Because you know ya girl just like I do. There's no way she's going to be calm and cool about the situation. She's going to go in guns blazing and kill him. Then there will be no way we can prove the truth to my father." He broke it down to me again like I was a toddler that was hard of hearing.

He was right and I knew it, but it just didn't sit right with me. "Okay, I'm going to do this with you, but if shit don't work out the way you say, I'm going to shoot you, Antonio, and your father, and we will just take our chances against the cartel. Do you understand me?" I asked, looking him straight in the eye.

"Yea, I hear you. Let's just keep our fingers crossed," he replied as he pulled his phone out and got ready to put part one of the plan into motion.

Chapter Twenty
Antonio

"Five hundred thousand dollars," I finished counting the money I had been slowly but surely misappropriating from the crew and the cartel. That, plus the other five hundred thousand dollars I had saved over the years was enough to give me a fresh start. I was done being the running boy for Jorge. For years I had done everything that he asked, to get virtually no rewards. I'd had no promotions, no raises, nothing in over ten years.

Ring, ring, ring. I grabbed my phone before it could go to voicemail. Glancing at the screen, I expected it to be my cousin in Miami. The same cousin who had planted the idea in my head and the same cousin who would be helping me to leave the country. Before I left though, I was going to attend the meeting Jorge had called for two days away. I knew what this meeting was about, but the negroes who had been pushing Jorge's dope had no clue.

After scanning the screen, I noticed it was a number I didn't recognize. I almost didn't answer. Realizing there was too much going on not to, I reluctantly hit the accept button.

"Hello," I said hesitantly.

"Hey, Antonio." I couldn't directly place the voice.

"Hey, who is this," I replied getting straight to the point. I had no time for bullshit. I had some loose ends to tie up and the caller was preventing me from handling my business.

"Hey, Antonio, this is Ivory. Can I come over?" There was no surprise that she knew where I was staying, because I was staying in a house that was owned by Schina's real estate company. What was surprising was that she had my number. I had only dealt with Nicole the whole time I had been there. I would expect Schina to have my number but not Ivory.

141

I almost told her no, but then I realized I needed to act as normal as possible. Of course she would be calling. My original Queen contact was now laid out on a slab at the neighborhood hospital. "Yea, it's kind of early though. Can I ask what you need of me at seven in the morning, Ms. Ivory?"

"Oh, I just want to do a little talking. I'm on my way. I have a key so don't shoot me when I come in." she laughed but I didn't. I had never considered the fact that they would have a key. I was slipping.

I tried to play off my unease by laughing along with her. "Ha ha ha. I wouldn't shoot a woman as beautiful as you. As a matter of fact, I never got a chance to give my condolences to you and Ms. Schina for the loss of your friend. I am very sorry that we could not save her."

"Actually, that's one of the things that I wanted to discuss. I will be there in about twenty minutes. Do you smoke or drink, Antonio?" I was even more intrigued with what she could possibly want. It seemed to me Blacc would be the one that she would want to talk to, but I just shrugged it off.

"I smoke, Ms. Ivory, as long as it's not what you Americans would call, dirt weed." I joked with her trying to ease my own nerves.

"Oh no, Antonio, I am a Queen. Surely, you know I don't smoke any bullshit. Well, anyway, I have a few blunts rolled already. I will see you when I get there." I stared at the phone for a few seconds as the screen displayed called disconnected.

I quickly came to my senses as I realized I needed to stash all of the money that was currently spread all over the dining room table and the kitchen counters. I hurriedly stacked it in the blue tote bag I had been stashing it in before I shoved it under the bed. I tried to straighten the house and make it look normal. Just as I was finishing up, I heard the key turn in the lock.

As I turned and watched her enter the house I was temporarily calling my own, I couldn't stop my jaw from dropping. I had never seen any of the Queens in anything less than their feminine version of gangsta wear, jeans, capris, t-shirts, tennis shoes, and usually in all black or white. That day, Ivory was standing in front of me wearing a purple strapless sun dress that swept her ankles. It managed to flow and hug all of her curves all at the same time. Her long hair was in bouncy curls that brushed her back. On her face she wore big square framed purple sunglasses. She was absolutely stunning. It didn't hurt that she was my type. I loved a big-boned white girl, with long hair, and all about her business. The goddess in front of me, though, managed to put all of my exes to shame.

"Antonio, hey," she greeted as she fully entered the house. "How are you?" Still staring at all of her glorious curves, I was momentarily speechless. "Antonio," she called, finally snapping me out of the trance her body seemed to have me in.

"Yes, oh, I'm sorry. I'm good. You look... Amazing," I responded for a lack of better words. I just hoped I didn't come across as sounding too corny, or thirsty as I had heard the Americans say.

She laughed a beautiful laugh before placing a soft hand on my arm. "Why, thank you, Antonio. It's been a long time since I've heard someone give me such a compliment."

"Well that means these American men you are used to are complete fools," I responded waving her on into the living room. I let her go ahead of me so I could watch the rhythmic sway of her hips. It was enough to hypnotize even the strongest of men.

"Well, come on, let's smoke a little and I will tell you what's on my mind, okay," she said as she had a seat on the cream colored couch.

"Yes, tell me what's on your mind and what brings you to my humble borrowed home," I joked with her as I had a seat next to her.

"Well, there's a lot that I want to know and discuss. Do you have any other plans for today," she asked with a beautiful twinkle in her eye.

"Nope, I am all yours, bonita," I replied. Of course, I did have other plans, but they obviously weren't ones that I could share with her.

"Good," she replied as I watched her reach in her purse. Having done so much dirt in my time, I immediately tensed up. Damn, I knew I should have... I never finished the thought as I watched her pull out a bag of pre-rolled blunts. "Let's smoke while you tell me what the hell happened in South Dallas."

We smoked two blunts while we went over and over what had happened. Finally, after I had told her the story four times, she was somewhat satisfied. "Well, it's definitely going to be some trouble in South Dallas. We know who the female is that was with them, and she won't be causing any more trouble, but now we have to find the rest of the snakes on the team. They must all be exterminated."

I watched as she lit another blunt. I didn't know how much longer I could hang. Even though I had portrayed myself as a smoker, I really wasn't and I was beginning to feel the effects. I could barely keep my eyes open.

"I just have one more question. Did you know that Blacc and Nicole were fucking?" My eyes shot open as I felt her hand creeping up my thigh.

"Ummm," I managed to mutter. She was slowly unzipping my jeans.

"Come on, Antonio, let's take this party to the bedroom." I damn sure wasn't going to put up a fight.

I jumped up off the couch as fast as I could and answered her question all at the same time. "Well, no, I didn't know for a fact that they were fucking, but I had my suspicions."

"Well, it doesn't even matter now, does it? That bitch is dead," she said cruelly speaking of her deceased friend. "Now, it's time for me to have a little fun of my own."

"Yes. Yes. Let's have some fun of our own," I agreed as she grabbed me by my hand and pulled me into the yellow decorated bedroom I had been sleeping in since coming to Texas at Jorge's command.

Once we made it to the bedroom, she roughly began pulling my pants to my ankles. God, I was glad she had already unbuckled them. "Antonio, do you want me as bad as I want you," she whispered in my ear, causing my dick to stand at full attention.

'Yes. Oh yes," I responded as I felt her hand wrap around my manhood.

"Good, I'm about to suck this dick and make you feel good, okay? I want you to fuck my face, like this is the last nut you will ever get. Do you hear me, Antonio?" I just grunted in return as she indeed dropped to her knees in front of me. I was going to follow her directions and fuck the shit out of her mouth.

Ssss was the only sound I could make as I felt the warmth of her mouth as she seemed to swallow it in one gulp. "Damn, girl."

I watched as she pulled my dick back out of her mouth and spit on it, using the spit as lube and jacked my dick slightly before placing it back into her mouth. I began to grind against her face as she went further and further down my dick. That was one of the reasons I liked white girls so damn much. They could suck the skin off a dick. She began to tug at her nipples through her dress as I did exactly as she asked, fucked her mouth.

I loved watching the shining of my dick as it slid in and out of her hot mouth, and when she deep throated to the bottom of my dick and then stuck her tongue out and began licking my balls, I thought I had died and gone straight to heaven. This bitch was the truth. If I didn't already have plans to get the fuck on, I would wife her ass, solely on her dick sucking skills. Just as I began to feel the tingle in my balls, she began to hum and I felt my knees get weak.

Again she pulled my dick out of her mouth, looked me straight in the eye and said, "I want to feel your warm cum shoot down my throat. Can you manage that, daddy?"

My only response was to grab the back of her head and shove my dick back in her mouth. Yea, I could make that happen for her. I was fucking her mouth so fast and hard, I was sure her mouth was going to be raw by the time I got done. Just when I thought she had pulled out all the stops, she tightened her jaws and let slobber run from her mouth.

"Oh, shit," I said giving her just what she wanted. All of my unborn children. It felt like I was cumming for hours and she stayed right there on her knees taking every damn drop. Not only did she take every drop, swallowing in deep gulps, she stared me in my eyes the entire time.

Just as I was pulling out of her mouth, having drained myself, I felt a sharp prick right between my toes. I was momentarily confused until I looked down and saw an evil grin on the hoe's face. In her hand was a syringe dripping with a clear liquid.

"What the fuck have you done," I roared just as I began to slide to the floor in front of her.

"Don't worry, it's just truth serum. It won't have any long term effects. As a matter of fact, when you wake up from your nap in a little while, you won't remember a damn thing, you fucking thief." My eyes widened as I saw Blacc enter the room right behind her. I couldn't help but to wonder how the hell they had figured it out.

Chapter Twenty-One
Money

I couldn't even pretend I wasn't excited about Schina being pregnant. And even though she had cheated, there was no doubt that was my seed. I just hoped that with her being pregnant it would help me to get my family back. I knew without a doubt she could handle being a single mom, but I was hoping that she would want our kids to have a two parent home and want it bad enough that she would somehow manage to forgive me for all of my bullshit.

"It's going to be a junior," I said to Schina as we were headed to the mall. It had been so long since we had done anything as a family, we had decided to make a trip to Grapevine Mills Mall. The girls loved LegoLand and we all loved to eat at the Rainforest Cafe. It would also give us a chance to do some school shopping for the girls, since we hadn't had the opportunity to do so at the beginning of the school year.

The night before, after getting the girls settled in Tai's room, Liv was too scared to sleep alone. Luckily, she was fine having a 'slumber party' with her sister. That made shawty and I debate for hours on whether to put them back in public school. She wanted to homeschool them, especially since she had decided after the meeting with Jorge, she was completely done with the streets. I was dead-set against it. I felt the girls needed the normalcy as well as the social interactions public school had to offer. She felt they needed to be close to her so that they could feel safe and loved. I think it was really for her. We finally just left the decision up to the girls and they both wanted to go back to school.

I knew their mom had to be feeling some kind of way, but it made me proud that we had raised them to be as resilient as they were. Nothing was going to stop them from doing what they wanted to do, and to me, that was a sign of good parenting.

As we finally reached the mall, I looked at my wife and saw her staring at our daughters in the rearview mirror. I reached out and grabbed her hand with mine, and even though I felt a slight stiffen in her body, at least she didn't snatch her hand away. "They're gonna be just fine. We have raised two very strong and very smart young ladies. Now let's just enjoy this day." I made sure to speak quietly so my words would only grace her ears, but as I looked back, I saw Tai watching us intently. "What's up, baby girl?"

She hesitated, glancing at her younger sister before replying. "Nothing, dad. But can we park by JC Penny's? I want to get some pretzels before we start shopping."

"Ooh yea, I haven't had any Aunt Annie's pretzels in a long time. Is that okay with you, mom and dad?" Liv, of course, just wanted to make everyone happy, but she damn sure wasn't going to pass up a chance to get some snacks on the way.

"That's fine with me," Schina responded. "That means I can stop at that candy store and get some Jelly Belly's." She was rubbing her hands together in pure Schina fashion. I was just glad this time it was behind something positive and not because she was planning something sinister.

"Wit' y'alls ole greedy asses," I said as I found a parking spot not that far from the JC Penny entrance. I wasn't going to lie, though. I was just feeling good that things were going well, at least at that point.

As we all piled out of the truck and into the mall, I noticed a few people stop and smile at us. I knew we looked good together and we were all decked out, too. Schina and the girls all wore white capris with jerseys supporting their favorite players. Tai had on her #43 Sproles jersey, she loved him since she played peewee football for the Eagles and also sported jersey 43. For the day she was rocking some green white and black Air Max. I wasn't sure how she was talked out of Js for that day, but I was glad that she had been. Liv had on her #88 Dez Bryant jersey, and some silver, blue, and white Air Max. That girl swore by Dez and the X. My gorgeous other half had on her #43 Troy Polomalu jersey. Retired or not, she loved her some big haired Troy, and of course she had on black, yellow, and white Air Max. And daddy, well I had on a custom Cleveland jersey the girls had made for my birthday the year before. It had the number one and sported the name "Money". I completed my outfit with some white True Religion shorts and some orange, black, and white Air Max. We looked good and we knew it.

"C'mon, daddy, let's go get pretzels while Mommy goes and gets those nasty jelly beans." I looked down and saw Liv tugging at my hand.

"Anything for my loves," I said as I winked my eye at her. We headed off to the pretzel stand as Schina went to get her "nasty ol' jelly beans." Every time we came to the mall, she had to get pounds of them. The girls and I couldn't understand her fascination with them. We just didn't understand the concept of food flavored jelly beans, but hey, we didn't have to eat them.

After grabbing our initial set of snacks, we headed to Lids. Everyone wanted hats to match their outfits, and I was determined to put smiles on everyone's faces. I knew the trip was about to set me back a grip, but it was going to be money well spent.

* * *

We had been in the mall for hours and we had hit Burlington, Forever 21, Justice, Nike, Journey, Foot Locker, and all the girls' other favorites, plus a long trip in LegoLand. I was ready for some real food and it was just in time because I could hear the roar of the alligator that was in front of Rain Forest Café.

"Ooh, c'mon, Liv, let's go put our name on the reservation list," Tai grabbed her sister's hand and ran off, knowing how things worked at the restaurant.

"Our babies are growing up," Schina said with a hint of sadness in her tone. "And I can't believe they are handling the whole Shawnta situation so well. I can't help but to wonder when and how it's going to affect them."

While she was never one to really worry, knowing she could control most things around her, when it came to our kids, she could be overbearing. Everything that went on in their lives was planned to a tee. I think that's why it was so easy for her to cut off her mom.

Thinking of that whole situation made me realize we hadn't discussed that whole situation and it had seemed to pass by with no repercussions. I knew Schina's mom all too well, so we needed to find out what was going on with her. "Not to change the subject like what you are saying isn't important, shawty, but what's up with your mom? Have you heard from her?"

She scratched her head and shook it all in one movement, before she gave me a reply. "Nah, not only has she not contacted me, she seems to have disappeared off the face of the earth. I want to say I don't care, but in all actuality, I do. I've actually had Blue out on the prowl for her. He's been…"

I cut her off, "Blue! What the fuck, Schina? That's not your boy. That's *my* best friend." I thought on it for a minute. "Well, I guess if I wasn't so busy doing my own thing, I would have realized you had him over on your side. Hell, I know I didn't bond his ass out, and I learned first damn hand if you don't want a person free you can make that happen," I said, referring to how she had left my ass sitting in the county, just because she felt like I needed it.

She actually had the nerve to laugh before she replied to me. "Yea, well you deserved that shit. And yes, I did bond him out, as well as made his charges disappear. He had no business sitting in jail because you are a hoe."

I really didn't want to go there with her so I quickly went back to the topic at hand. "Anyway, back to your mom before we ruin a great family outing."

She gave me the side eye before she replied. "Anyway, I wasn't going to punish Blue for your disloyalty. But, yes, back to my mom. I don't know what's up with her but I'm worried. I just hope me keeping the kids away from her didn't lead her back to a life of drugs."

Before we could dwell any further into the conversation, our bright eyed children had run back to us. "Fifteen minutes," they yelled in perfect harmony.

"Okay, well let's go in the bookstore while we wait." That was typical Schina. Always on the hunt for a new book or twelve to add to her immense collection.

I couldn't even front, she had gotten me addicted to street lit and I didn't mind adding a few books to the collection as well.

***

It was later that night and we were all exhausted. Schina and I were laid in the bed together and I was damn sure about to at least try to get me some pussy. "Shawty, look, I know things haven't been right between us. I know I didn't step up as your husband and the girls dad when I should have. It's just that damn video really fucked with my pride. No matter what, I always knew I could say no one had touched my pussy in all of the years we had been together. Seeing someone else…"

"Just stop, Money. First, I know you just wanna fuck. Second, I can't tell you what our future holds. All I know is right now our girls deserve to have their family. They need all the normalcy that they can get. Honestly, it's the only reason you are in my house and damn sure the only reason you are in my fucking bed. I'm not ready to have sex with you, plus I'm tired."

"What the fuck does that mean, Raschina? 'Cuz if you think I'm going to stay here now, just for you to put me out later, you got life all the way fucked up."

"Money, just take your ass to sleep. We can deal with this later. Right now, I just wanna sleep." She must have taken me for a fucking joke.

Chapter Twenty-Two
Schina

It was Monday morning, and I was up getting the girls ready for their first day of school. I was still very skeptical of them going, but I had lost the vote and now there was nothing I could do but deal with it. I was kind of hoping Money and I could at least take them together, but he hadn't been home since Saturday night when I wouldn't give him any pussy.

There was no telling where the hell he was and, to be honest, I didn't have the time nor the energy to worry about it. Surely by now he could see that all of his extracurricular hoes had bad things happen to them, so I could only hope he was in one of the rental properties jacking off.

"Mom, where's dad?" Tai seemed to bring my thoughts to life. "Yesterday you said he would be here to take us to school, but now it's almost time to leave and he still isn't here."

My body was rocked with a bad wave of nausea as I tried to think of an answer to give her. "I don't know, my love. But we still have about fifteen minutes before we leave," I responded, hoping against hope that he would show up in time. Not only did I not want to disappoint the girls, I also wanted him to be there to keep me calm as I tried to register the girls for school.

"Why did he even leave in the first place?" Liv decided to pitch in.

The day before, when we woke up and he wasn't there, I knew what it was, but of course I couldn't tell the girls the truth. I just told them that he needed some time alone because it hurt him that as a daddy he didn't protect them. It was the best I could come up with as their eyes watered over the cinnamon pancakes I had cooked for breakfast yesterday.

"Well, here is some good news, though. Even though y'all have missed two weeks of school, tomorrow is a staff holiday and there is no school tomorrow. Whether daddy is home or not, I thought we could go to Wal-Mart and pick out some new things for y'all's room. I thought it might be time to change what our rooms look like." I was hoping I could bribe them into smiles. And it worked. On Liv.

"But, it won't be as fun without dad. And plus, he said I could have that new bed and stuff and you know you can't build anything, mama." Tai was back to her old throw salt in mama's game type of ways.

"Well, if Dad isn't here, we will just go buy the furniture from a place that will deliver it already set up. Now grab your backpacks," I said, pointing at the backpacks full of supplies that the girls and I had bought yesterday. "It's time to go."

As we drove to Tosch Elementary, which was actually out of our district, I let the girls' favorite station play. The girls had been going to the same school since Kindergarten and I paid a hefty ass fee so they could remain there.

As we pulled into the driveway of the school, I saw Money's black on black Charger and I was glad he, at least, wasn't shirking his daddy duties. "Look, girls, daddy is here."

As we climbed out of my car and headed over to him, I let my mind wander, trying to decide if our relationship was even worth trying to save at that point. I knew we had a lot of shit to talk about and a lot of pain to try to get over. I just didn't know if I had it in my heart. Not to mention I had to plan the home going of one of my best friends. I had the meeting with Jorge about Lord knows what, and I had to find a way to break it to my crew that I was leaving the streets alone. My plate was too full for his bullshit.

"Hey beautiful ladies," Money said, kissing each of us on the forehead like he slept with us the night before or some shit. I shot him a look as I led the way into the school.

"I'm good, daddy. I just hope I don't have to go to P.E. today." Of course, Liv kept it sweet and simple. She never let shit get to her.

"Where have you been, daddy? I wanted to play the game with you yesterday," Tai said, speaking of the PS4 we had bought while we were at the mall Saturday.

"Ahhh, I'm sorry, babe. Maybe, tonight."

Before Tai could even respond I butt in, "Probably not tonight, either. The girls are going home with Janet. We have that meeting. But if you want, you are more than welcome to go to Wal-Mart with us tomorrow to pick out new bedroom decorations," I offered solely for the girls' sake.

"We'll see," he responded halfheartedly.

Getting the girls enrolled went a lot smoother than I had anticipated and I appreciated it because it gave me time to call Laurelland funeral home and start the process for Nicole's funeral. With everything that had taken place, I hadn't even had a chance to go to the hospital and view her body, and I was feeling terrible.

Once I had given them my credit card information and let them know what I wanted and not to worry about the cost, I decided to spend the rest of the day pampering myself, so I called Ivory to see if she wanted to join me.

"Hey, hoe," I greeted, sounding way more cheerful than I actually felt.

"Um, no, that would be your husband. Or Blacc. Or even that tramp that's laying in the morgue. But not me," she replied back. And as cold as her words were, the bitch had the audacity to laugh.

"Damn, bitch, tell me how you really feel," I said as I, too, couldn't help but to laugh. "But anyway, I was wondering if you wanted to go with me to the nail shop."

"Yo' ass is crazy as fuck, yo!"

Her answer took me by surprise so I stared at my phone for a second before I asked, "What? What I do now?"

"Bitch, your kid just shot one of your husband's ex hoes, you have a meeting that you have no idea what it's about tonight, your man's a hoe, and your home girl's laid up in the morgue, and you want to go get your nails done?"

I thought about it for a minute before I gave a reply. "Well and my toes and maybe my eyebrows, too." I normally didn't give two fucks about no damn eyebrows, but I was ready to try something new.

Ivory laughed uncontrollably for about five minutes before she responded, "Honey Nails on Ferguson?"

"You know it, bitch," I responded as I turned my car in that direction.

***

I was watching the Vietnamese lady who always did my nails as she buffed them when I realized I had never told Ivory about the meeting with Jorge. "Bitch, wait. How the hell you know about that thing tonight? I never called and told you about it."

"Bruh, don't think you are the only one with connections. I not only know about the meeting, unlike you, I know what the meeting is about. I don't have an official invite, but I will be there. I'm also bringing a guest and a special gift."

"Oh, so we keep secrets now?" I asked with my burning ass eyebrows. Hell, I might not know what the fuck that meeting was about, but I could promise I'd never let another bitch wax my fucking eyebrows. Hell no, I'd just have to live with my fucking unibrow. That shit hurt and I wasn't down for unnecessary ass pain. Well, except tattoos.

"Bitch, you can't say shit," Ivory said louder than was called for, making the two other women that were getting their nails done look in our direction.

"What the fuck y'all looking at," I asked, more ready to start some shit than admit that she was right. I watched as they hurried up and put their heads down. We had been coming here for years so the nail techs already knew how we got down. They didn't even flinch, just kept right on buffing or whatever the hell they were doing.

Ivory just looked at me and laughed as she shook her head. She knew me well enough to know I wasn't going to willingly admit to being wrong. That's why she was my ace, she knew me all too well. "Anyway, bitch, so is your husband back home or what?"

I sighed as I shook my head. "Well, that nigga *was* home."

"*Was?*" She snickered and even the damn nail tech looked at me like she was crazy.

"Yea, hoe, *was*. But then the night we went to the mall his ass thought I was just about to fuck him like he ain't been laid up with half the damn thots of Dallas over the last fucking month. Tuh, who the fuck he think I am? So when I told him I wasn't giving him no damn pussy, his ass got up and left."

"So, did he bring his ass back or what? Don't play. Just tell me what the hell happened."

"Hell nah he ain't bring his no good ass back home. As a matter of fact, I ain't see his ass again until this morning at the girls' school."

I guess she decided she didn't even want to know anymore because she changed the whole damn subject. "So did the school trip about the girls not having been there over the last two weeks?"

I thought of all the money I had dropped that morning to fudge the records. "You know money makes the world go around."

"You know one day you're going to get yourself in a situation that money ain't going to get you out of."

"Bitch, I guess you forgot my kids were just fucking missing for three damn weeks, huh," I retorted with attitude that wasn't even really her fault. But she just kept touching on issues she knew were going to be touchy. Hell, she knew better than to hit me with everything at once. "That's also why I will be telling Jorge I'm getting out of the game. I'll pass this shit down to you, Money, and Blue if y'all want it. But me, personally, I'm tired of all the extra shit that goes along with it."

It seemed like for once in the duration of our friendship, I had rendered her big mouthed ass speechless because she didn't say a word. She just stared at me with her mouth hanging open.

"What? I knew you didn't think I was going to do this shit forever. If there's any sign that it's time to let it go, it's the fact that my kids were kidnapped."

"Yea, but they weren't kidnapped because of some street shit. They were taken cuz your dude's a damn hoe that invites drama into your life like it's a damn Christmas present."

I couldn't help but to laugh at her silly ass. "Yea, that's true, but if I wasn't always running the damn streets worried about this and that, I'd always be at home with my babies and no one could snatch their asses, right?" I said. For the first time since I had made the decision, I started to second guess it. She did have a valid point. Aside from a few shootouts, there hadn't been much street drama. From the looks of it, even when we began expanding, it went fairly smooth. "Nah, bitch, you almost got me. But, I'm done. I'm ready to be a stay at home mom. Between the real estate company, the catering company, and all the other companies, I'm set for life. That's not even including all of the money I have saved up over the years. I'm even thinking of starting a publishing company. I'm good on that life."

"Well, you know I'm behind you whatever you decide to do. Guess I'll move closer to you, that way you can keep Danyelle, cuz I'ma get it how I live til I can't live no more."

We both got silent and I knew we were both thinking of Nicole, she used to say that dumb shit all the time. "You know I got J. Speaking of Danyelle, is she home now?"

"Yep, my Baby Cakes got home while y'all were doing the fake ass family shit Saturday. I know if Garland is out of school tomorrow, then Mesquite is, too, let's get the girls together."

I just nodded my head as my nail tech finally finished up and waved me over to the dryer. Damn, I swear I loved time with my best friend.

***

It was later that evening and I had received the text from Jorge. The meeting was, ironically, set for the same warehouse I had killed the father of my deceased son. I couldn't help but to question how the hell Jorge had access to some shit I owned, but I guess when you're the head of a cartel you had access to just about everything.

Since I wasn't exactly sure what the hell was going on, I decided to keep it gangster, classy, and flexible all at the same time. I decided on another suit that I had custom fit to my curves. That night I opted for a midnight black Tom Ford suit paired with the matching Tom Ford heels. The shoes had gold embellishments so I decided to wear a shiny gold shirt under my suit and of course I had to rock a black and gold Tom Ford tie. I put my hair up in a quick bun, sprayed myself with Beyoncé Heat and hit the door.

As I slipped my key in the door to lock the house, I heard a car pull into the driveway. I quickly pulled Beauty from the holster that was very nicely concealed by the cut of my outfit. I didn't have time for any bullshit. I wasn't going to show any fear though, and went on to lock the door. As I smelled the sexy ass Jean Paul Gautlier, I knew the only danger I was in, was sliding out of my panties, so I slid my baby back in the holster and turned around to face my husband.

"Look at you, trying to match all this smoothness," he chuck- led as he gave me a once over. Almost as if we had planned it, he was also rocking all black and gold. Wearing an all-black suit, black shirt, and gold tie, he was turning me the hell on and I knew we had to get a move on or I would go back on all that hot shit I was just talking a few nights before. He would be all up in my guts and not only would I make a liar of myself, we would be late for the meeting.

I knew that couldn't happen so I just snapped, "What are you doing here?"

He didn't even pay my question any mind, instead he walked up and rubbed my still flat stomach. "I figured, since we didn't know what was going on, it would be best if we at least made an attempt at showing solidarity."

After knocking his hands off of me, I replied, "Don't touch me. I don't know who else you've been fucking touching. But because I don't have time to debate with you, we can ride to- gether."

He laughed because he knew that was really my way of say- ing he was right. "Well, come on. We might as well take the Charger, it matches our outfits."

I shook my head and just headed to his car. It wasn't even worth the argument. "Whatever, Byron. Let's just go." As soon as my ass hit the seat, I put in the Boosie C.D. that was in my purse.

"Shawty, don't nobody wanna hear that bullshit." He always had to say something, couldn't ever just go with the flow.

"Well, I do. I would be listening to it if I was in my own ride, so just let me listen to my C.D. and think, okay."

I was glad for once he had gotten the point. I didn't want to go there with him. I needed to focus on what the hell was going to happen at this meeting. I knew if Jorge had brought his ass all the way to Dallas, it couldn't be anything good. Add that to the fact that Ivory was showing up with who knows who or what and my ass was definitely on edge.

I reached in my purse and grabbed a blunt. "Oh hell no. Shawty, you straight tripping. First, I know you ain't smoking weed while you carrying my seed. And I know you not about to try to smoke in my car."

I stared at his ass like he had grown a second head. "Nigga, you have a better chance of harming the baby with some random ass STD since you wanna try to come home and fuck me after your dick been everywhere. And how you gone care more about this fucking car than your own health. I swear I will never understand your simple ass."

I guess he had had enough of my shit though, because not only did he eject my C.D. and throw it out the window, he snatched the blunt out my hand and threw that out, too. "Look, man, you gone quit treating me like I'm some fucking lame. Maybe if you handled me like a fucking man, I would keep my ass home. And if you call me anything besides boo, Money, or Byron ever again, I'ma go upside your fucking head, Raschina Marie. Do you hear what I'm saying to you?"

"Let me tell you something. If you ever put your hands on me again, I'm going to send you home in a goddamn box. I don't know what the fuck you think this is, Byron." He must have left his damn mind wherever he spent the last two days. I sure hoped he went and picked it up soon.

"You know what? I'm going to let this go for now. But only because we need to go in this meeting and act like we are as one. But, go ahead and text Janet and tell her the girls are staying the night. We gonna hash this shit out as soon as this meeting is over."

I started to argue with him about it, but I realized that one way or another we did need to figure out what the hell we were doing, so I just did as he asked.

The rest of the ride to the warehouse was silent, and I was glad, even though I really wanted to pull out another blunt. I just wasn't willing to let another one fly out the car, so instead I just stared out of my window at nothing.

Once we pulled up to the warehouse, I was glad to see the soldiers that I had called on standing around waiting on me, dressed in all black just as I had specified. I knew there was no way we could win a war with the Salazar Cartel, but I damn sure wasn't going out without a fight. That just wasn't in my nature.

Just as I waved at them to follow me in, I heard the heavy rattle of bass pulling up behind me. Before I even had a chance to pull my own heat, my crew had circled me and pulled their own. And just that quick, for the second time, I wondered if I had made the right decision in stepping down. How could I walk away from all that loyalty?

As I peeked over the shoulder of Skeet and Chris, who of course had placed themselves directly in front of me, I saw it was none other than my best friend dressed in all white. That wasn't the kicker, though. Her ass had Blacc in tow. Oh boy, this was about to get very interesting.

Chapter Twenty-Three
Money

I watched as everyone swarmed my wife. I wasn't sure how I felt about the fact that I wasn't even given the chance to protect her, but I guessed like everything else, I had brought that shit on myself. I just turned like everyone else to see who was pulling in. My mouth dropped open as I watched Ivory and Blacc hop out of the big body Excursion that had just pulled to a stop in front of us. Not only was I surprised to see them together, but the fact that they were both dressed in all white really blew my mind. How the hell did that happen? Hell, if she could forgive that nigga then shit, my wife needed to forgive my ass, too. Yea, I had done more shit, but I never fucked her friends. And we damn sure had more history. Tonight she was going to hear me out and I was going to get my damn family back.

"Well, look at this shit," I heard Schina say. "Oh, this must going to be real good. Okay everyone listen up. To be honest, I have no idea what this meeting is about or why he called me here. I am aware that someone in the crew does know, and hopefully has it under control, but for once, it's not me. All I can say is let's not go in here acting like this is a damn western. If I feel the need for a showdown, y'all know I have my ways of letting it be known." I admired her as all eyes were riveted on her. I knew as a man it should be me giving this speech, and hopefully, once she stepped down, I could earn the same respect that they gave her. But for now, I would follow her to lead. She took a deep breath before she continued. "To be perfectly honest, all of us might not make it home tonight."

"Well, we can damn sure bet your fine ass gone make it home," one of the crew retorted. The funny thing is, it wasn't even sarcasm. These men were willing to lay their lives down to make sure she walked out of the warehouse in pristine condition.

Hell, I couldn't even be mad about the fact that all eyes were on me because whoever spoke called my wife fine, right in my face.

Though I wanted to act an ass, I knew that without her word, I would most likely die in that parking lot, so I just shrugged. "Hey, it is what it is. She's fine as fuck," I responded, gaining a round of laughter.

"Y'all let's be serious. I know y'all will die for me, just as I will die for you guys. And all I can promise is that if one of us doesn't make it, I will make sure you go home in style. And you know your families will always be taken care of. As long as there is a crew, they will be straight. For those of us who do walk out of here, I am calling another mandatory meeting Friday night." She glanced at the pink pearl face Movado on her wrist. "Okay, guys, it's show time."

As she turned and walked to the door, we all started behind her. I couldn't help but to admire the sway of her hips as she led us into the lion's den. Dude was right. My wife was fine. And I wasn't ready to let her walk out of my life.

"Hello, Raschina," Jorge greeted from the head of the board-room table that had been placed in the center of the warehouse floor. The fact that he called her by her first name, and not mija, automatically put me on high alert. I could tell it also unsettled her by the way her back stiffened.

Even though she wasn't comfortable, she never wavered in her steps, though, walking to Jorge and placing a kiss on his right cheek. "Hola, Jorge," she responded as she took a seat to his immediate right. Seeing as the seats to his left were filled, with what I could only assume to be his heaviest hitters, Ivory, Blacc, Funky, Skeet, Chris, and Chase all sat to Schina's right. I slowly let my eyes scan the warehouse and I could see that he had many men placed in strategic places around the warehouse. I also watched as the remaining crew members spread out as well. Shawty had them well trained, but while we seemed to have them by numbers, I'm sure the fire power that he had spread around far outweighed ours. There was nothing to do at that point but hope for the best.

"I'm glad you all could make it," he said staring at Blacc, and putting emphasis on the word *all*. "*Son,* don't you think you should be here by your Papa's side?"

"Well, *Papa,*" Blacc shot back using the same emphasis on the word papa, "in the short amount of time that we have been in each other's lives, the number one thing you have taught me is to be loyal to those who are loyal to me. You have also taught me that if someone proves to have your best interest at heart, you should be willing to lie and die for them. For me that is the crew over the cartel. And that is why I chose to sit with Schina, Padre."

While I expected Jorge to get all hot-headed, instead he gave a short head nod and turned back to wifey. "Well, Schina, it looks like no matter where you go, you earn respect and loyalty. I commend you for that. Before we get to the matter at hand, you do know, Antonio, correct?"

Everyone looked on in surprise when Ivory responded in place of Schina. "Oh yes, the Crew knows Antonio very well." I could tell by the glint in Schina's eyes that she knew something was going on, but I could also tell by the way she held her body that she had no idea what it was.

"Your right hand speaks for you? You are agreeing that you all know who Antonio is, Schina, Money?"

I didn't like that he threw me in there, but I knew to play my part, so I simply nodded my head, letting my wife continue to assume her position as our speaker. "Yes, Jorge. I am aware of who he is. I haven't spent much time with him, considering the majority of my time since I was released from the hospital has been spent searching for my children. But I know who he is and why he is here."

"Oh how inconsiderate of me not to ask of the wellbeing of little Liv and Tai. How are the girls?" he asked. His voice sounded as if he genuinely cared, but I doubted at that moment it was as important to him as he wished it to seem.

"The girls are fine. I don't mean to seem disrespectful, Jorge, but the crew has many internal issues that need to be resolved. I know that it must be a very important reason that you have flown to Texas, so let's cut to the chase, shall we?" I had to respect the balls that my wife was displaying, but I couldn't help but to wonder if it was said balls that would lead to our demise in the drafty warehouse we were seated in.

"Ahh, yes, always about business. Okay, let's cut to this chase that you speak of. Antonio here has been a part of my inner circle for many years. It was to my surprise when he came to me a few days ago and brought it to my attention that the Crew had cheated me out of hundreds of thousands of dollars."

"What?" I almost didn't recognize her voice as Schina stood letting her chair slide several inches behind her. As I turned to look at her, I noticed multiple red dots appear in strategic places on her body.

"Fuck," I said out loud. I could only assume that the guys she had brought with her noticed them as well because the silence was broken by the sounds of many hammers being pulled back.

"Stop. Stop. Everyone calm down." I was shouting above the humming of the blood in my ears, to me it sounded like a mere whisper.

"Call your men off, Schina, or my men will shoot." It was at that moment that Schina, too, noticed the lasers spread across her body. She never panicked or got upset, simply raising her hand signaling for our guys to stand down. "Now, have a seat so we can talk about this while I decide on who is to pay for this."

I wasn't really expecting her to do as he said because it just wasn't in her nature, but surprisingly, she did so. Locking eyes with me and then Ivory as she did.

"Jorge, one thing I can stand by is that no one in my crew is a thief."

"Are you willing to bet your life on that?"

I watched as her eyes scanned the people in the room. If there was a thief amongst her people, it would be someone in this room. Of course with the exception of me, because I had been missing from crew activities and Nicole, of course, no one else would have access to large amounts of cash. "Yes. Yes, I'm willing to put my life on that, Jorge. Now why don't you tell me exactly what you are accusing us of before we go any further and maybe we can figure it out."

I had to admit, I was proud of her. She was being exceptionally calm about the whole situation, especially knowing if no understanding was reached, regardless of what was said outside those doors, she wouldn't be going home to our children. I was admiring how high she held her head when she reached out and grabbed my hand. It was then that I realized she was nowhere near as calm as she portrayed. The tremble in her hand was enough to make me want to pull my pistol and put a bullet in the old man's head. I didn't appreciate anyone making my wife feel like that, even if she momentarily hated me.

"Antonio, grab the bag, please," Jorge directed the smug faced asshole sitting next to him. It was like the whole room stood still as we all watched him walk to a bag we had all missed. It was a blue nylon over the shoulder duffle bag and it was sitting right between Schina and Jorge. Everyone seemed to gasp as he unzipped and dumped the bag into the center of the table. Bundle after bundle of money fell on to the table.

I saw Schina shake her head in confusion as she stared at the money laid out in front of us. "I'm not understanding. If this is the money my crew supposedly stole, why are we sitting here wasting time that I could be spending with my children?'

We all waited not so patiently to hear whatever answer the old man was about to spit. He let us sit there staring at him like he was crazy as he reached into his pocket and grabbed one of the cigars he had seemed to always be smoking while we were in Mexico.

"Because, Mija," he replied with an unnecessary amount of sarcasm. At least to me it seemed unnecessary, and judging by the squeeze she gave my hand, Schina did as well. "This money in front of you is counterfeit."

Shawty did the most unexpected thing after he said that. She threw her head back and laughed. While all the men on the opposite side of the table stared at her like she was crazy, those on our side sat back in our seats, discreetly placing hands on hidden weapons. I wasn't sure exactly why she was laughing, but I knew that meant she was probably about to come out the side of her neck. We all knew that, it's why so many hands were reaching for pistols.

"So, you mean to tell me, you think in the midst of waiting for me to awaken from a coma, looking for my children, dealing with inner circle disloyalties," she shot her eyes in my direction as she said that last part and all I could do was lower my head, "and expanding our territory and everything that goes along with that…" She let her voice trail off as she tried to stop her giggling. "You think in the midst of all that bullshit, we had time to learn about making counterfeit money. Ha, ha, ha."

"This is absolutely no laughing matter," the cartel head said as he raised his hand and the red dots were covering my baby's body again.

This time as they were also met with pistols pointed in their direction, Schina didn't stop what was going on. "Listen, Jorge, I don't know exactly what's going on, but as I said, I will put it on my life that my crew had no parts of any theft. This," she eyed the money on the table, "looks to be a half a mil, am I correct?"

"I'm impressed. That's exactly what this is," he responded with a knowing smirk on his face.

"Well, even before we started dealing with you, this was chump change to my crew. Well, at least to those of us who would have access to it, just as I am sure it is to you. So that means the leak is somewhere between the pickup location and the drop-off location." The conviction in her tone was enough to make me believe her, but I wasn't the important one.

"Yes, you are correct. A half a mil to me is nothing. I just bought a yacht for more than that. It is simply the principle of the matter as I am sure you understand. And for you to try to place the blame on my side of the table, is rather," he paused as in thought of the correct words, "ballsy of you to do, no?"

"Yea, maybe it is," I could hear the attitude I had been expecting, finally rear its head as she responded to him. "But that's just what that is. My people didn't take your fucking money. You need to take a look at the people around you. I stand by mine. The question you should ask yourself is do you stand by yours?"

"And what does that mean," but just as he asked the question, it became evident what she meant. Just as there were red dots dancing all over her body, they were dancing all over his as well.

"Now, yea, your men may take me out, but I can promise mine will take you out as well, and the difference between the Crew and the Cartel is, the Crew has many heads. If you take me out, the Crew will continue to thrive whereas the Cartel will fall. Now, do you want to talk about this rationally or we just gone shoot this shit out?"

I could tell he wasn't used to facing such ultimatums, and I'm sure it made it worse that it was coming from a woman. He paused for a few minutes as he pondered the situation he was in before he raised his hand, calling his shooters off. But to the room's surprise, Schina didn't follow suit.

"Are you not going to call your men off, too?"

"Nope, actually, I'm not. That is twice that your men have virtually threatened my life behind some shit that I'm telling you I had nothing to do wit..." She didn't get a chance to utter another word before Jorge himself pulled a pistol and shot her in the center of her chest.

Chapter Twenty-Four
Ivory

I was hurting way more than I thought I would be. I mean me and her were never as close as Schina and I. Then the day she died, I found out she was betraying me. But nonetheless I missed her trifling ass. I missed how she always seemed to be the calm in the midst of our chaos. While Schina and I were shoot first ask questions never, she was always a find out the details kind of person.

I laughed as I thought back to the day Schina killed V. We had made a bet that Schina couldn't go in and kill her without all that extra shit. I just knew for once she was going to be able to do it, but nope. Of course she couldn't.

"I knew this bitch wasn't going to stick to the plan. Pay up, bitch. Hell, I ain't watching this shit. This shit is cheating. I ain't playing no parts in this shit. Ivory, you got this?" She had asked the question like she was giving me a choice, but then the hoe stormed out the room without giving me a chance to respond. I laughed even harder as I thought of how we fought all the way home because I felt like she owed me half the money back, since our horny ass partner didn't even bust a nut.

It, at that moment, crossed my mind that someone should probably check on Blue. While they weren't significant to each other, they had been fucking for a while before he got locked up. I knew for a fact that they were having phone sex while he was in. I started to grab my phone and call him when I noticed the time. I just didn't have time, plus chances were we would end up in the limo together. I'd just keep my eye on him then.

I finished my makeup and then looked at myself in the full length mirror that was mounted on the back of my walk-in closet door. I had to admit, I looked great.

According to the directions that were mailed to my house, everyone in the crew was to wear white and pink. We were wearing pink because it was Schina and Nicole's favorite color and we were wearing white because it was a celebration. We were celebrating Nicole's life and not mourning the loss of it. At least that's what we were all told.

I had decided on a white long sleeved maxi- dress. The pink wedged sandals I was wearing were one of the presents Nicole had given me for Mother's Day last year. I stashed my pistol in the pink clutch that matched the shoes. I had curled my hair in long spiral curls and used a matching clip to hold it back out of my face. I smiled as I thought of all the times she had told me she loved my hair in this style. All of that was topped with some shiny pink lip gloss and glittery eye shadow and I was ready to go.

Just as I started to descend the stairs, I heard my doorbell ringing. I rushed the rest of the way down the stairs and looked out the peep hole to see who was ringing my doorbell that day of all days. I was surprised to see Blue standing there. I hurriedly swung the door open.

My mouth dropped open as I stared at him. "Damn, am I ugly or something," he joked as I stood there staring like a crazy person.

"No, it's not that... It's..." I didn't even know what to say.

"It's that you're used to a nigga being a gangsta and you didn't realize I could be a GQ gentleman, right?"

I laughed as I pulled my door closed behind me. "Yea, I guess you could say that." I had to admit he damn sure looked good. He had an all-white tux and some white alligator shoes. His shirt was white with thin pink pinstripes and he wore a matching pink tie. It looked real good against his dark skin. If he wasn't so far off limits, I might would let him sample my honey pot, but I had never been a trifling ass bitch. I damn sure wasn't going to start the day we laid my friend to rest.

172

"I can't even take credit for it," he said as we started walking side by side towards the white limo that was waiting by the curb. "From what I understand all of the pall bearers had the same suit delivered. That's some boss shit when you can get a niggas measurements without him even knowing." He was shaking his head as we made it to the limo and he held the door open for me.

"Yea, you know how that goes. She's not really the type to risk someone messing up her plans, now is she?" We both laughed as I climbed in the limo and smoothed my dress out.

"You damn sure right about that. Man, Ivory, I didn't think I would miss her crazy ass this much," he said and I could even hear the tears in his eyes. I knew we were both about to cry and I was glad I didn't put on mascara or eye liner.

Sure enough, we spent the rest of the ride reminiscing on our fallen soldier. We laughed, cried, and I think I even yelled a few times, but by the time we pulled up to the funeral home, we had managed to pull ourselves together. As our limo pulled into the circular drive, I saw four other limos pulling in as well. I knew that would be the Captains as well as the head of the crew.

I admired the decorations that were even placed outside. Schina had definitely gone all out for our girl. There were caged doves placed by the front door, as well as pink balloons and pink tulip and rose bouquets.

As I was helped out of the limo by the driver, I looked back and saw Schina being helped out of her limo as well. When I saw my girl, I couldn't help but to flash back to that night at the warehouse.

I had been waiting for the perfect moment to make my little presentation and it was too late. "Why didn't you act faster," I thought to myself as I watched my best friend, my sister, my ace grab her chest and collapse to the ground. It was like the whole room had went into shock. While I expected it to sound like a war had erupted, it was silent except for that nigga Money yelling like he was the one that was shot.

I jumped up from my seat, staring at Jorge and yelling all at the same damn time. "You better hope she's not dead or I'm killing your bitch ass, your hoe ass son, and your thieving ass right hand man. I put that shit on my motherfucking daughter, bitch nigga. Y'all don't let that nigga or the bitch that dumped the money make a mother fucking move. I swear if they do I'm airing this bitch the fuck out."

I had finally made it to Schina and to my amazement, I didn't see a drop of blood. "Bitch, I ain't stupid. If it ain't a headshot, I ain't going out." I didn't know whether to laugh or cry, but I knew it was time for me to take the floor.

"Bitch nigga," I said pointing a finger at Jorge and my pistol at that snake Antonio, "you got the game all fucked up. You shot the wrong motherfucker and I promise if my niece or nephew don't make it, I will rain hell on you."

Jorge looked as amazed as me by the fact that Schina was now sitting up. "You need to watch how the fuck you talk to me," he said pointing a finger back in my direction, "before I make sure the next shot is a headshot."

"I meant every word I said. Just like my sister said, the snake is in your own fucking front yard. Blacc, can you pull the god damn projector screen down so we can show your punk ass daddy what really went on."

Blacc didn't even bother to reply. Just walked to the corner where we had stashed the projector and screen that held the evidence to clear the crew of any wrong doing.

"I promise this better be good or both of you bitches will be laid on a slab with that other one," Jorge said. I could tell he was highly pissed off by how strong his accent had gotten, but I didn't give a fuck. I was beyond pissed my damn self.

As soon as Blacc was finished getting everything set up, he went and stood behind Antonio with his pistol pressed tightly against the back of his head. I was sure that Jorge would want his own revenge against him, but my bitch had taken a bullet for his ass and he would go on our terms. Fuck them and their rules.

"What is this, Sherry," Jorge asked, calling me by my government.

"Just fucking watch, and if you still don't approve of what's taking place, then me and my sister will both pay the fucking consequences," I said, pulling Schina to her feet. I helped her to a seat before I pressed play on the remote Blacc had tossed my way.

On the screen was a relaxed Antonio sitting in the same house I had sucked his dick in. I cringed at the thought, but it was definitely worth it.

"So, Antonio, why did you do it?" Everyone could hear my voice very clearly. I guessed Jorge knew where this was going because his body visibly tensed.

"Because I'm tired of being Jorge's damn fetch boy." The manner in which he answered showed his true feelings. You could hear all of the anger and disdain that he had been carrying around for however long.

"What the fuck is a fetch boy?" I was making sure to ask questions to show that these were his true thoughts and feelings. I wanted to leave him no way to weasel out of a damn thing.

"Go get this, Antonio. Go get that, Antonio. I've been in the same position within the cartel for years. I've had no promotion and I damn sure haven't gotten a fucking raise. I was tired of it and it was time for me to find my own damn way." Because of the Pentothul I had administered to him with the syringe he had seen, he was very relaxed and had no problems telling us exactly how he felt. Things had gone exactly as I planned.

"So instead of doing all of this extra shit and causing drama between the Crew and the Cartel, why didn't you just go to Jorge like a grown ass man?" That was a question, I hadn't thought to ask and I was glad that Blacc was there to catch that slip.

"I did try to go to him. He told me that your ass would be the next to be promoted. You just come waltzing your bastard ass into the picture and everything that I have done for him over the years no longer make a difference."

I could tell that he was getting drowsy, but I had two more major questions to ask before I let him sleep off the drugs. "So how much money have you taken from him over the years and how the hell did you manage not to get caught?"

Again he didn't hesitate to answer. It almost seemed as if he was boasting by then. "I've gotten away with about a mil over the years. Every time he has me come to the states on a mission like this one, I would take a portion and pad the rest with counterfeit money that I had gotten from my cousin."

I finally hit the end button and turned to stare Jorge in the eyes. "And you almost killed my fucking sister behind some shit your dude did. There will be restitution, I can promise you that. And the first thing will be this," I said and snapped my fingers.

Boom! I watched as Antonio's brain matter splattered all over Jorge. I snapped my fingers again and watched as all of Jorge's hidden men were marched out, each having a pistol to the back of their heads. I watched as our men sitting at the table rose and went to their side of the table and placed pistols to the back of their heads as well. It was almost like this part of the night had been planned. The only one sitting safely was Jorge. He would walk away safely, but only because we couldn't stand an all out war with him.

"Which one of these men can you not live without," I asked still staring him right in the eye. Once he shrugged and put his head down, I made eye contact with one soldier and set the whole *thing in motion. One by one his men were slaughtered. "Never underestimate a bitch with a lot to lose," I said to Jorge as I resumed my seat.*

He spent the rest of the evening pleading with Schina to forgive him. And I sat there watching, knowing there was more to the video, but only one other person's eyes would see it.

Misty Holt

Chapter Twenty-Five
Schina

Nicole's funeral was packed. There were so many people in attendance, some had to stand. I watched in disgust as Blue and Blacc cried over her bogus ass. All I could do was shake my head as I turned my eyes back toward the front where her body rested inside a pink and white casket.

I regretted that the casket had to be closed but, due to her face and body being literally shredded to pieces by bullets, an open casket viewing was not an option. But I had made sure to have her favorite selfie blown up and placed atop the casket. There were so many pink and white flowers, it smelled just like a floral shop.

I knew balloons weren't typical for a funeral, but I didn't care. Nicole had expressed to me during a girls' outing a couple years prior that she loved balloons. She had told me how she could never have enough of them. I felt it was my job to make sure she took plenty of them home with her.

My thoughts were broken by the sound of the preacher's voice. "I would not say to you that everything is all right. Because it's not and you know it. You hurt. And we know you will hurt for a long time. God made us so that we can have relationships with one another, and when that relationship is lost, we feel pain. You have lost a loved one - and it hurts.

"Yet, I would like to speak a word of comfort today. It comes from John 14:1-6, where it says, 'Let not your heart be troubled. Believe in God, believe also in Me. In My Father's house are many dwelling places. If it were not so, I would have told you. For I go to prepare a place for you. And if I go and prepare a place for you, I will come again, and receive you to Myself, that where I am there you may be also. And you know the way I am going. Thomas said to Him, 'Lord, we do not know where You

179

are going, how do we know the way?' Jesus said to him, 'I am the way, the truth, and the life. no one comes to the Father, but through Me.' From this passage of scripture I find three thoughts of comfort."

The sermon seemed to go on forever, and my attention began to wane. After what seemed like an eternity, I finally heard the moment I had been waiting for. The long-winded pastor ended his message and called me up to speak.

I held my head up high, walked to the front and grabbed the microphone. I cleared my throat theatrically, and then spoke from the heart, knowing that what I was about to say would send shock waves throughout the room.

"I would like to thank you all for coming out to help us wish a happy homecoming to a trifling ass bitch." A cacophony of loud gasp echoed off the walls. But i wasn't fazed. "Yea, I know. You all were expecting me to get up here and talk about what a wonderful person this bitch was. But everyone knows, I'm too damn real to lie, no matter where I am or what the circumstances are. I brought this lying, conniving, trifling ass bitch into my family, only for it to be brought to my attention that she is the one who helped set up the kidnapping of my children. For two weeks, I cried and searched this city looking for my children and this hoe," I punctuated my statement by shoving the casket which held that disloyal ass bitch. That quick but brutal shove sent the casket and her cold, stuff body crashing to the floor. The lid popped open and the body rolled out onto its side.

I looked down at Nicole with no remorse.

"Oh, my god!" someone cried.

"Don't feel sorry for that fucking snake! She knew where my kids were all along," I spat. "My biggest regret is that she didn't die by my hands. I would have done that shit slow and painful. She was jealous. She was a thief. And she was a snake. Someone I can hold no respect or love for. Now I know some of you are probably feeling some kind of way. And for those of you who are, I will let you see the evidence. For those of you who stand by me, let's roll out."

I threw the microphone down and walked over to her body which was still lying on the ground. I was glad, too. That was exactly where it deserved to be. As I looked down upon her, I hocked up the biggest wad of spit I could muster and launched it at her body, watching it splatter against her forehead. Fuck her.

As I walked back down the center aisle, I could sense the crew following behind me. We were going to do exactly as I had said. Have a damn party.

***

It was later that night and me and the crew were holding down the VIP section in a popular strip club in Dallas, Club Onyx. Everyone was drinking, smoking and having a good time. Everyone except me, of course. Money was watching me like a hawk. If I even looked at a blunt too long, he acted an ass. It wasn't even worth the fight to me. Besides, the morning sickness had faded, and I really didn't have an excuse anymore, anyway.

Watching everyone party and carry on, I thought back to the video that I had left the rest of the folks watching at the funeral home.

Antonio was still sitting on the couch, but he was slightly nodding off at this point. Slap! Ivory reached out and slapped the hell out of him and he lethargically reached up and rubbed his jaw. Even across the screen a red palm print was already visible.

"Why did you slap me," he asked just beginning to slur his words.

"I need you to answer just a couple more questions, so wake your hoe ass up." Her mouth was damn near as bad as mine nowadays. *"Now, you say you have been doing this off and on for years, obviously you have never went to Jorge and pointed out that a drop was short. Why would you do it now?"*

"Because Nicole told me to." The first time I heard those words my heart almost stopped. I had stood up and walked to the screen in my media room, where Ivory had shown me. I stood there with my chest heaving up and down like I could fight what was by then a dead man.

"What the fuck are you talking about?" You could tell that she, just like I, was hoping he was lying, but we both also knew under the circumstances there was no way.

"Yep. We been fucking since I got here. Not only was it her idea for me to tell him, she is also the one who set it up for your boss's kids to get snatched while in Orlando."

The video went on to explain the how and why she did what she did, but none of that was even important to me. The thing was this bitch had my kids kidnapped and tried to get me killed because she wanted to be the head of the Crew. Hell even if I would have been killed that night in the warehouse, she wouldn't have gotten the reigns.

The only thing that confused me about the situation was if she had helped to cheat us out of five hundred thousand dollars, why would she go shoot it out with some niggas over a punk ass five thousand dollars? I figured she only did it because Blacc knew that the money was short. She had to make everything look normal. I wasn't really sure, and since the loose pussy hoe was dead, I would probably never know, but I was okay with that.

As I decided it was time for me to head home, I realized then was as good of a time as any to tell the crew my news. I had all the captains in one place, so I could save us a little time.

"Hey, can I get everyone to come closer. And send the strippers away for now, please."

As everyone did as I asked, I sipped from the bottle of water I had ordered from a damn near naked waitress. "What is it, boss lady? I'm trying to get me some ass from that fat booty bitch I just had in my lap," Chance said with laughter in his voice.

"Well, y'all know we have done big things together. We have seen a lot of shit and made a ton of money. What y'all don't know is that I'm pregnant." I raised my hand to silence them as cheers of excitement and congratulations were tossed around. The men were all patting Money on the back like he had made the baby by his damn self. "Thanks guys. But, I've decided it's time for me to step down. Time for me to leave these streets alone. After almost losing the girls to some bullshit, I just can't do it anymore. I can't risk the lives of my kids."

Just as I expected, Funky was the first to speak, "While I can respect your decision, boss lady, what does that mean for the rest of us?"

I looked around at all of the expectant faces and realized I was really going to miss my crew. "I can't answer that. As of now, Money is the person that you all need to talk to. Of course, with the way we parted with Jorge, a new connect is needed, but if Money is willing to man up and lead you, then it's his. If not, of course Ivory will be handed the offer. Hell, I don't care, they can run this shit together. All I know is I'm done."

I heard a lot of groans and carrying on but at that point, I didn't even care. I got up and passed out hugs and got my things, ready to head home.

As I passed my husband, he grabbed my arm. I almost snatched back, but I had been trying real hard to be civil with his ass, plus I had just passed him the torch. "What, Money?"

He gazed into my eyes and it was almost like old times, before all of the deceit and drama he had brought into my life. "Are you headed home?" I just nodded my head in response. "Can I come home with you?"

"Your name is on the deed. I can't legally stop you."

"I really want to talk to you, shawty. About a lot of things, but if you're not in the mood, then I will just go back to the townhouse."

Oh that's where he was staying, in the townhome, well the only one he knew about. I actually owned five of them, and the only one I wasn't making any money off of was the one he was residing in. Oh well, at least he wasn't shacked up with some new pussy throwing, money chasing hoe.

I thought on it for a second before I nodded my head. "Yes, I guess we do have a lot to talk about and tonight is probably as good as any. Come on."

That worked out for me anyway because I had ridden to the club in the limo with Ivory and Blacc. I was planning on calling an Uber to take me home, but I wouldn't have to after all. I knew Money had driven himself.

As we exited the VIP, everyone hugged me once again and congratulated us both on the baby. I know I heard at least five people say they expected to be named the Godfather. I didn't even acknowledge that. Ivory would be the sole Godparent, just as she was with the girls.

I let Money grab my hand and lead me towards the exit. A part of me didn't even feel like dealing with him, but deep in my heart I still loved him. I just couldn't decide if our good times outweighed the bad. He went in this relationship knowing what kind of woman I was and he totally disregarded that. And I had gone completely against my own principles by forgiving him, more than once, for cheating. I just didn't think I could forgive him again. But, I knew either way it went, we had to try to work something out for our children. We at least had to figure out how to co-parent.

One thing I couldn't take away from Money was that he was a damn good father. Well, at least until recently anyway. The only time I had ever doubted his parenting skills was as I was running the streets looking for our children, and he was out doing who knows what. But the girls had no idea it had gone down like that and, as far as I was concerned, they never would.

"What you thinking about, shawty? You're way too quiet and we all know that ain't you," he joked as we climbed into his car.

"Just thinking of all the shit we have been through, and where the hell we are supposed to go from here," I answered honestly.

He grabbed my hand again and stared into my eyes as he spoke, "Babe, I know I've hurt you. I know I have. And I know I can never take that pain from your heart, but hopefully I can begin to rebuild your trust. Hopefully, I can make you fall in love with me all over again. But let's just get out of here and go home and talk, cool?"

I thought back on how much I did used to be in love with him and how good it felt. "Okay, boo. But, I'm going to call in an order to the Denny's off of Lake June, cuz I'm starving," I said rubbing my stomach. "What do you want?"

"You know your man well enough to not have to ask that question," he replied as he turned the key in the ignition and began backing the car out of the parking lot.

Yea, he was right. I did know him. I knew all of his likes and dislikes just as he knew mine. Was I ready to let that go? Was I ready to try to build that bond with someone else? How long would it take before I trusted someone else enough to let them into my heart? All of those thoughts were racing through my head as I placed our usual order. I didn't have the answers to any of those questions, but I was willing to at least hear him out.

I stared out the window, slightly bobbing my head to the slow jams playing on 105.7 as he steered the car towards Denny's. "Money, you really hurt me, man."

He was silent for a few minutes before he responded. "Yea, shawty, I know. I'm not going to sit here and try to make up some bullshit ass reason on why it happened, either. I don't know. I guess it was an ego thing. The attention those hoes gave me made me feel good."

"Ego? Attention?" I was confused. I could promise on everything I loved that no one gave him the attention I did. "I don't get what you are saying, Money. I dote on you. I try to cater to your every need. I treat you as the King I am supposed to treat you as. What are you saying?"

"Babe, let's just wait until we get home and eat. Hell, I might even let you hit the blunt for this conversation." He chuckled as he said that.

I looked him upside his head as he said that. It just let me know he was probably about to be on some bullshit.

Chapter Twenty-Six
Money

I didn't really want to let her smoke, but I was willing to do whatever it took to get her to be calm and listen to what I had to say. I truly loved my wife and I *needed* to go home. I had been staying in the townhouse for the last few days and life just wasn't right without my wife and kids. I couldn't sleep right without feeling the warmth of her body. I was tired of eating out and I needed to hear the laughter of my daughters. I knew I had said it before, but I was ready to get my shit together and do right by the ladies in my life. With Schina being pregnant, I needed to be there on an everyday basis.

As we drove home in silence, I had decided to save my words for when we got home. I thought about what she had just said at the club. Of course she had already told me she was ready to leave the streets alone, but I hadn't believed her. For the last few years, she had run the crew damn near by herself and I knew she loved the thrill of it. But what surprised me even more, was the fact that she said she would be handing it down to me and Ivory. I wasn't sure how that was going to work. It was bad enough being bossed around by a bitch I was married to and fucking. I knew Ivory was going to feel she had the right to do the same damn thing and I wasn't having it. She was going to have to fall in line. I also needed to consider whether to try to repair shit with Jorge or find a whole other connect. There was so much to consider and I knew the best advice I could get would come from my wife, another reason I needed to make things right between her and I.

Once we were in the house, Schina immediately went to the kitchen to get plates. We would eat in the living room, by her suggestion. That alone was a surprise. She was very anal about her house and usually food was restricted to just a couple of rooms. I just chalked it up to her being pregnant.

Once she had returned from the kitchen, I admired her beauty. Even in the tailored men's suit she was rocking, her curves were on full display. Her ass was so round and plump, jumping with every step she took. And now that I knew she was about to gain that baby weight, I couldn't get my dick to mind his own damn business.

"That's why we even need to have this talk," she asked as I tried to discreetly adjust myself. I should have known she was going to notice. She knew me too damn well. Too well, that's why I couldn't figure out what the fuck my problem was. I needed to be loyal to my wife cuz no-one was going to love, respect, obey, and please me like the beautiful bossy woman in front of me.

"Schina, I know there aren't enough words in the English language to convey to you how sorry I am. I know there is no way I can take back all of the pain I have put you through."

"Nope, there's not. But you know what, Money? My biggest reason for not being as willing to forgive you as usual has nothing to do with who and where you've been dipping your dick. Do you know what it is?" I guess she could tell by the look of confusion on my face that I was at a complete loss. "Don't worry, I'm not going to leave your simple ass over there guessing. Hell, there are too many indiscretions for you to let your brain cycle through, now aren't there?"

I wasn't trying to let this get ugly, so I debated on whether to address her blatant disrespect. Knowing I was going to have to start putting an end to all of that shit with her and Ivory, I decided to go ahead an address it. "Look, shawty, I know I done fucked up, but whether we get back together or not, whether you let me come home or not, you're going to have to stop talking to me all crazy."

Surprisingly, she just nodded her head before she spoke again. "You're right, because regardless, we have to raise these children together," I watched her rubbing her non-existent belly as she went on. "I don't want my daughters thinking it's okay to disrespect their husbands, and if this is a boy, I damn sure don't want him thinking it's okay to have a disrespectful ass woman. But anyway, let me get back to what I was saying. The one thing that completely pushes me away from you is…" She let her voice drift off and got a look of pure rage on her face.

"Nah, we ain't gonna do that either. I know you are capable of expressing yourself without all of that." All I knew was I wasn't trying to get my ass shot, and that look was usually followed up by bloodshed.

I watched as she reverted to her breathing techniques, and while I would normally be talking shit, that day I decided to let it go. "I don't understand how pussy was more important than our daughters. While Tai isn't your blood, you have raised her as if she was. And Liv, our baby, that's all you, bruh. How could you not even bother helping the crew look for our children, Byron?" I was surprised when the look of anger was replaced by a look of sorrow. I was even more surprised when she broke down in sobs. I started to get up and try to comfort her but she quickly threw one of those petite hands up. "I don't want you to touch me right now. I just want you to give me an explanation that I could understand. I mean, you were the reason that I, *their mother*, couldn't be out there looking. So don't you think that you, *their father*, should have been?"

She wanted an explanation to make her understand, but I didn't have one of those. I put my head down and took a couple of bites of the food we had abandoned. I really didn't want it at that point, I just needed a moment to think. What was I supposed to tell her? I finally decided to just keep it as real with her as I could. Not enough to die over, but enough for her to realize even I was ready for me to change. "Baby, I'm not going to sit here and give you no lame ass excuse. I can't. It's beyond time for me to start keeping it a hundred with you. It wasn't that I didn't worry or want to find our kids."

"Well, what was it then, boo?" The look on her face let me know that this was going to be one of the most crucial things I've ever said to her.

"It's because I was feeling like less of a man. I knew in my heart if you weren't laid up in that hospital, you would have found her. I knew that, just like what happened, that it would be you and your lil posse that rode in to the rescue. I don't have the reach or respect of the streets that you have. So I ran to something I knew would show me respect. Sex. I know that these streets bow down to you and they give you what you want. But Dallas doesn't love nor fear me like it does you, or even Ivory."

I watched as my wife's shoulders slumped. I could only hope it was in understanding and not in defeat. "But we discussed that in Mexico, Byron. You have to take control of the streets. You can't run every time the heat is up and expect anyone to give you respect. The streets respect me and mine because we make them. I make these streets bleed when they against me. You go disappear in some pussy."

"Yea, I know we talked about it. I know that. But honestly do you think if I would have come back without you by my side, and nutted up it was going to mean a thing to Dallas? It wouldn't have. Especially not under those circumstances. I had just put one of their beloved Queens in the hospital. Hell, I couldn't even get respect from the crew. Out of the hundreds of people you control, I could only get thirty to follow me. How the hell was I gonna get people outside of the crew to tell me a damn thing, Schina? I'm still a man. A man with pride and that shit fucked with me." She started to speak but I wasn't through. "No, wait a minute, hear me out. I know it was wrong as fuck to let my pride come before my family, before my kids, but that's what it is. Baby, I'm sorry."

"The thing is, I'm tired of hearing 'I'm sorry, baby.' I'm tired of having to worry about whether my man is sticking the dick to someone else. I'm a good woman. Just like I have the respect of the streets, I deserve the respect of my husband. You don't give me that. I'm tired, Money. Do you know when I found out I was pregnant, before I could even decide if I was excited about the baby or not, I had to make sure your ass hadn't given me a damn disease. Do you know how embarrassing that is? How fucked up it is? No, of course you don't. Just like I don't want my daughters thinking it's okay to disrespect their husbands, I also don't want them to think it's okay for their husbands to disrespect them. And with you running around fucking all willy nilly, that's exactly what they are going to think. While we can hide it from them now, one day they are going to realize what the hell is going on. I will not let my daughters sit around and cry over some bullshit. I won't." I had to respect what she was saying. That was a very valid point that I had never considered. I just hoped it wasn't too late to save my marriage.

Chapter Twenty-Seven
Ivory

I was getting dressed for the meeting Schina had called for later that day. I was making sure to be extra careful with my appearance because this meeting would serve two purposes.

She was holding the meeting in a club that she secretly owned. I don't think anyone knew she owned it except me and that trifling, and dead, hoe Nicole. She would be holding the meeting early in the evening. She said she had chosen the club because the whole crew would be there and it was the only place she could think of where it wouldn't look suspicious to have over two hundred crazy ass niggas chilling at one time. Then after the meeting, we would be having her 'going away' party. So, I guess it did make sense. I just hoped no one acted up because I would hate to have to come all the way back home to change.

I looked in the mirror, as I finished my makeup. My face was beat to the Gods as usual. I wore a smoky grey eyeliner and mascara. My eyeshadow was dark purple with a touch of the grey at the corners of my eyes. I rocked a clear lip gloss that had a slight purple tint, and it was all brought out even more by the fact that my hair was pulled up in a messy bun.

But my outfit, that's what took the cake. I wore a dark purple chiffon dress that reached my ankles. But while the dress was long, the slit that went from my left ankle damn near to my pussy print kept it from being too conservative. Add to that the plunging neckline that showed off my perky double D's and you couldn't tell me shit. I stood up and admired the way the dress hugged all my curves just right. I was sexy as fuck, but not slutty. I loved it.

I had just sat down on the bed to buckle the grey and purple wedge heels I had purchased on my last shopping spree with the bestie when my phone rang. I grabbed it off my pillow and answered. I thought I sounded as sexy as I looked, "Hello."

"Bitch, bye! Who you waiting on?" I laughed when I heard Schina. I knew she was gone have some shit to say, just like I knew it was her ass on the phone.

"Nobody, hoe. Is you here?" I asked, reverting to a ghetto girl tone.

"Yep, the limo driver is about to ring…" Ding, dong.

"My doorbell, right now," I finished for her and started laughing. "Okay, let me get my shoes on and grab my purse and I'm on the way down."

"Okay, with your slow ass. I know you got some weed. Bring a blunt. For some damn reason, I have 'morning sickness' again, and I cannot go into this meeting throwing up and shit."

"Okay, but this is the *last* time, Raschina Marie, and I ain't playing with you."

"Whatever hoe, just come on."

I finished buckling my shoes and grabbed my purse and the blunt out of the ashtray before heading down. Once I got to the door and opened it, I was surprised to see Chris standing there. "Damn, bruh, she got you on driver duty?" I asked before I started laughing.

"Nah, I refused to let y'all be driven by anyone else. Especially with her being pregnant. Too much shit been going on, ya know?" I noticed that the whole time he was answering me he was scanning my body. I also noticed the look of appreciation in his eyes. To hide the blush I felt crawling up my face, I hurriedly turned to lock my door.

As I turned back around, I let my eyes crawl over his body, too. I also appreciated what I saw. He was wearing an all-black linen Gucci outfit and he was looking too damn fine. If he wasn't a virgin…

"Get your ass in the car, hoe." I was brought out of my thoughts by Schina's loud ass mouth. I looked over and realized Chris had somehow made it to the car and was holding the door open. Both he and Schina were staring at me with smirks on their faces.

I just lowered my head in embarrassment and walked over to the car. I almost jerked as Chris grabbed my hand. "I just wanna help you in, Ivory. You good?" Chris asked, causing Schina to burst out in gales of laughter.

"Nah, she ain't okay. You got her panties wet," she said in between breaths.

"Shut up, bitch," I said as I finally climbed into the black limo she had rented for the night.

"It's all good, Ivory. You made my dick hard, too," Chris responded with humor as he closed the door behind him.

***

It was the next day and I was thinking of how well the meeting and her good-bye party had gone. Surprisingly, only a few had grumbled about Schina handing everything down to Money and I. To be honest, I was one of the few to grumble. I just didn't understand how she felt that us two were going to work well together. I had no respect for that hoe ass nigga, but for my best friend, I would at least try.

I needed to be getting up because I was due at Schina's house in a little over an hour, but I had a raging headache. For some reason, the night before, every time I had seen Chris dancing with someone else, I would feel the need for another drink. I was paying for that shit, too. I didn't know why I was feeling him all of a sudden, especially not enough to be stressing who he was spending time with. But there was no denying it. I would mull over it, but right then I just didn't have time.

I climbed out of my bed and went to my closet. I was glad that my closet was neat and organized because I needed to leave the light off for as long as possible. I reached in and grabbed a pair of white shorts. *"Good, white,"* I thought to myself. That meant it didn't matter what color shirt. I had seen a pair of white sandals as I stumbled through my house the night before. Those small things made me smile. I just had no energy for any planning, so I reached in to the t-shirt side and grabbed a t-shirt. I was glad to see it was the Dallas Cowboy shirt Danyelle had gotten me a couple of years before. That would mess with Schina's nerves and I was down with that.

I turned my shower on and went to wake up Danyelle. It would be the first time got to see her friends since they had been home. I knew she was excited, but I had no idea how excited. Once I walked in her room and saw her fully dressed, I realized it had been too long. "Hey, Babycakes," I said, calling her the nickname I had given her at birth.

"Hey, mama." Her voice was full of happiness as I rubbed her cheek. "Is it time to go, yet?"

I laughed before I answered. I loved the way our kids got along so well. "I need to take some Aleve and jump in the shower. Then we will be out, babe."

"Yes!" She jumped up with joy and I chuckled as I headed back to my room. That girl kept me on my toes. She was so beautiful. My only concern was that one day she was going to ask about DB's bitch ass. I honestly had no idea what I was going to tell her. I knew I couldn't tell her the truth, but I would just cross that bridge when I got to it.

I had taken my shower and put my clothes on when my phone rang. I grabbed it as well as my purse, and headed to get my daughter. We needed to get the hell outta there and on the road. We were running late and Schina was going to be talking shit.

"Let's go. We are so late. Your aunt is going to be straight tripping," I said to my daughter at the same time I pressed answer on my phone.

"I damn sure am," my best friend's voice greeted me from the other side of the phone. "Why is your ass just now leaving your house, heifer?"

"Man, I woke up with the worst headache. It took me awhile to start moving around, B." There was no point in doing anything aside from telling her the truth, so I did just that.

"Whatever. I'll see you when you get here."

"Your ass must have got some, damn," I looked at my daughter who was walking slightly ahead of me. "You know what I'm trying to say. But yea, you must have slept good, cuz you are too damn cheerful."

"Nope, as a matter of fact, I did not. I just woke up feeling good. I can't wait to find out if I'm carrying a girl or a boy. I'm ready to do some shopping." When she said she was ready to do some shopping, I knew that her perky tone was a front. The only time she *wanted* to shop was when she had some heavy shit on her mind.

"I don't know what's wrong, best friend," I said to her. "But whatever it is, just like everything else, we will get through it."

"That's why I love you, Ivory. You are always worried about me. Even if I probably have caused more dirt than everyone we know, you still have my back. Ride Together," she started our mantra.

"Die Together. Bad girls for life." We always said Martin and Will's quote fit us, and it was our own motto. We lived and probably would one day die behind it.

"I'll see you when you get here, my nigga." *Click*.
***

After speeding over to Schina's and watching, or more so listening to, the extremely loud reunion between our daughters, we sent them to the game room. We had a lot of business to discuss and we were all ready to get down to it.

197

"So, what are we going to do about a connect," Money, of course, felt the need to speak first. I wanted to say something fly, but his question made a lot of sense, so I just let it go.

Both of our heads swiveled in Schina's direction, where she was sitting picking at her nails. I could tell there was a lot on her mind, but she and I would discuss the personal shit later. It took a few minutes for her to look up and see us staring. "What? I'm just here as a mediator. I have no say in what goes on in the streets. I'm just here to make sure y'all don't kill each other, at least not on my carpet. I'm thinking about selling this house."

Money and I just glared at each other. Neither of us was sure how to work together, but we knew it had to happen, especially if Schina was dead set against giving her opinion. After a long awkward silence, I decided to speak first. "Well, I can't say I don't ever want to work with Jorge again, but I can say I don't want to right now. I know who Daniel used to get his dope from. I'm sure he will deal with the crew."

"I agree with not working with Jorge for a while, but let's look for someone else before we go to that nigga's source. I had always heard he had some trash. I don't know if it's because DB stepped on it or if it came that way."

I pondered over what he was saying before I responded. "That's true, but since no one else has any weight around here, that we know of anyway, how about we do a trial run? Maybe just buy a kilo and see what it does. In the meantime, we can be looking for someone else, just in case."

I saw Schina nodding her head, but that should have been no surprise. We learned the game together so it would only make sense that we thought the same. "I know I said I wasn't in it, but, Money, her idea makes a lot of sense."

I watched his shoulders slump before he nodded his head. "Yea, I guess it does, but I sure hate having to resort to using that nigga's plug."

Even though I could feel where he was coming from, we were doing business. We damn sure couldn't keep letting his personal shit interfere with what we had going on. I was going to speak on that point, but I let it go for the sake of his wife. There was no doubt in my mind, though, that his shit would once again affect us all.

Chapter Twenty-Eight
Money

After we finished with our business talk, Schina decided to go lay down. I thought Ivory would grab Danyelle and go home, but she didn't. She said something about the girls and Belly and rushed off to the media room.

I decided to go check on Schina, she looked a little pale while we were talking. I was worried about her and the baby. She had been through so much and I knew it wasn't good for her. "Babe, are you okay," I asked as I walked into the master bedroom.

"Yea, I'm just tired." She was still looking pale, and that heightened the worry I was already feeling.

"You need to call your doctor. Now, shawty." I wasn't sure how my demands were going to go over, but I meant it.

"Yea, you're probably right." I was so ready for her to protest, I had already started the argument in my head.

"Shawty…" I stopped. "Wow. Yea, you must be feeling terrible. Let me get your phone before you change your mind."

I listened as she talked to her doctor, who must have told her to come on in, because she got up and started getting dressed. "He said come in, now?" I knew things had to be bad for him to want her to come in right then.

"Yea, can you drive me?" If I wasn't sure that she felt bad, that question made me realize how bad it really was.

"Of course. While you're getting dressed Ima go ask ya girl to stay with the lil ladies, then I'll come back and get you."

"Okay, Byron."

***

"Raschina, your blood pressure is way too high. I don't know what's going on in your life, but you need to get a handle on it." I put my head down as the doctor was speaking. I felt so bad because I knew I played a major role in that.

"I know, doctor. And I think I have most of it under control now. I just want to know if my baby is okay. The rest I will deal with as I have to."

"Well, let's take a peek at baby Morgan and listen to its heartbeat, okay?"

"That's cool, doctor. And this will be daddy's first time hearing it, too," she responded, sounding way more cheerful than she looked.

I thought back to her pregnancy with Liv, who was being promoted to middle child. It was so special. I was at every doctor's appointment. I was constantly rubbing on her stomach. We talked, sang, and read to the baby together. Now here she was almost two months pregnant, and I'd played virtually no role. I wanted this baby to roll and kick in her belly for me just like Liv did. Fuck the dumb shit. I was going home whether she liked it or not.

"Do you hear that, boo?" I had been so engrossed in my thoughts, I almost didn't.

As I sat there mesmerized by the *thump, thump, thump* of our baby's heart, I turned and stared into my wife's eyes. *I love you,* I mouthed, not wanting to interrupt the beautiful monotony of the heartbeat.

Schina merely nodded her head before closing her eyes. I was on the verge of getting pissed off when I saw the first tear trickle from her eye. It was knowing that I was the cause that made me rise to my feet. I hurried to her side where I tried to catch the tears. By then they were falling in steady streams and I was helpless to stop them. "It's all good, shawty. We gone be okay and so is our baby. I promise."

"Well, I don't know about y'all, but this baby is going to be fine," the doctor said, reminding us that he was still in the room. "But it's going to be dependent on some changes on your behalf, Mrs. Morgan."

"Just tell me what she needs to do, doc. I'll make sure it happens," I responded, reaching for Schina's hand.

"Well, it's a must that we bring that blood pressure down. I know she believes in going all natural while pregnant, but I'd like to prescribe methyldopa. It's been tested and shown to be safe. I think right now it's a must for her."

"Can y'all quit acting like I'm not sitting here, damn." That was much more like my wife.

"My apologies. And also, until your blood pressure is under control, I'm strongly suggesting bed rest."

I genuinely expected her to stand up and throw a fit, but she didn't. "That's fine. I'll get Ivory to come stay with me. Just write the script and let…"

I didn't even stay to hear the rest. I just stormed out of the examination room. I didn't want to hear shit else she had to say right then. She had me all the way fucked up. That was my wife and my baby, not no fucking Ivory's. I would be moving home, no matter what she had in her head. I knew it was going to be a fight, so it was a good thing he had prescribed her blood pressure medicine. Things were going to get ugly before they got pretty, that was for damn sure.

***

"Byron, I'm not ready to deal with you." We had fought all the way home and I was tired of it.

"Schina, I'm not asking you. I'm telling you. If you don't want me in the room with you, that's fine. I can sleep in the guest room, just like she can. This is *my* house, *my* family, and *my* baby. I *will* be here. If, after you have the baby, you still want me gone, cool. I'll be out. In the meantime, you *will* let me do what's right."

"Hey, y'all. You're upsetting the girls. I'm going to take them to get something to eat. Have this shit cleared up before we get back." I heard Ivory mumble something under her breath but didn't even try to respond. We both just nodded as she walked away with the girls in tow.

"Money, you are not moving back in my house," my wife said as soon as we heard the door close.

"First of all, this is *our* house. I can move into this muthafucka if I want to. And I am." I hated how much my fuck ups had ruined us. Even more than that, I hated how they had stolen her submissive side. She normally knew better than to contest me. I watched as she walked over to our closet. I thought she was going to put on something more comfortable, but she wasn't. Instead, she began throwing my clothes out.

"No, Byron. I'm done with you. I want you out of my house and out of my life. You can get the girls whenever you like, but you gotta take 'em to the townhouse. I want a divorce." By the time she made it to the end of her rant, she was screaming at the top of her lungs.

Divorce? What she thought this was, reality TV? Fuck a divorce. This shit was 'til death do us apart. If that's really what she wanted, I could arrange that, real quick.

I rushed to the closet where she was by then just leaning against the door. "Bitch, you got me fucked up. You want out of this marriage?" I asked as I snatched her delusional ass up by the neck. "I'll let your ass out."

I was so out of my mind, I didn't even feel her hands clawing at my arms. I also never heard the front door open and close. I never heard Ivory come up behind me, but I did hear the *boom.* I also felt the burning sensation in my body. Right before everything went black.

Chapter Twenty-Nine
Ivory

"Oh, my God! Oh my God!" cried Schina. We were sitting in the waiting room at Parkland and she was pacing back and forth. "I don't know whether to hope he's okay, or hope that he's not. I'm so confused!" She babbled.

I watched who I hoped was still my best friend as she sank to the floor. While I regretted bringing more stress into her life, I wasn't sorry I had shot that nigga.

When I ran back into the house, I had only intended to grab my phone. Once I was in there, I decided to see if Schina wanted anything back. Instead, I had walked in on a scene very reminiscent of the one in Mexico. I had pledged to put a bullet in his ass if he ever put his hands on her again. Me being me, I stood true to that. Now, there we were waiting to see if he was going to make it.

I took her by the elbow forcing her to stop pacing and look me in the eye. "Schina, I hate that it played out like that. But I couldn't just stand there and watch him hurt you again." I was hoping she would forgive me. But if she didn't, I was okay with that, too. At least she was alive. It was better to see tears running down her face than blood.

"Ivory, I understand why you did it. But I still love him. I can't help it." She wiped a fresh stream of tears that poured down her face.

"Well, I couldn't help what I did either."

"I understand. I would have done the same." She reached out to hug me and we embraced.

Knowing she didn't hate me took a lot of the pressure off my shoulders. I personally didn't give a fuck if his ass died or not.

As we broke our embrace, I saw a doctor emerge from the tan double doors we had been staring at. "Looking for the family of Byron Morgan," he called. Judging from the look on his face and all the blood on his scrubs, I assumed it was bad news. Just as I began to worry, I saw Schina collapse.

***

"Are you going to the hospital?" It had been three days and there was no change in Money's condition. Danyelle and I were staying at the house with Schina and the girls. It was not just my love for my sister but also the guilt I carried on my shoulders that made me want to be there.

"Yes." I knew beforehand that her answer was going to be short and curt. Even though she swore she didn't hate me, I felt a chill coming off of her words every time she said anything to me.

"Schina, can I talk to…" I didn't even get the question out before tears were streaming from her eyes. I was so hurt and confused. I had always been the one she turned to for comfort. I was always the shoulder that she leaned on. Now that I was the one to cause the pain in her life, I simply didn't know *what* to do.

"Girls, come on. I'll drop y'all off at school," Schina yelled at the children as she gathered the hot pink tote bag she had been using.

"I'll take Danyelle," I offered. Even though I had transferred my baby to the same school as the girls, I wasn't trying to push my responsibilities off on Schina, especially not at a time like that.

"Ivory, what I really want you to do is just leave me alone right now." I started to say something fly in return, but I knew that it was just pain speaking. We had been through worse and I could only hope we would get through that as well.

"You got it, Schina," I replied as I grabbed my baby on her way past me. "Give ya mama some love before you go Baby-Cakes."

As I hugged my daughter, I watched Schina's shoulders droop. I really wished there was something I could do to take away her pain, but I couldn't. I still didn't regret what happened, but I was feeling bad about not being able to be there for my best friend.

Chapter Thirty
Blue

I was struggling to accept the words the doctor had just said to me. *Months.* I'd never understand how they can look a person in the eyes and tell them something like that. As gangsta as I was, I could never carry the burden of telling another grown man that he would only live for days. *A year at the most,* he had said. But it wasn't like a nigga of my caliber was going to let another motha fucka tell me how long I was gone live. I would be the one to decide when my time was up.

I wasn't even thinking about that punk ass doctor as he put his weathered hand on my shoulder. I was too focused. I needed to talk to one person, and one person only—my nigga, Money. But he was still in a coma, just floors down, fighting his own medical crisis.

Regardless, I still had to go down there and hold holla at him before I followed through with the plan that had popped in my mind.

I looked up at the doctor and said, "Yea, okay, Doc. All I want to know is can I go see my brother?" I had been admitted into my own hospital room just the night before. A small, drab, sterile room that might as well have been a prison cell.

There would be no flowers or tear stricken faces standing beside my bed. I had no one. Nobody but Money, and he damn sure wouldn't be visiting.

I had known about my diagnosis for over a year. Cancer. The big C. I had opted out of chemo after the first few rounds, and I was paying a deadly cost. I had hidden the illness for so long because it made me feel like less of a man. There was no-one around to teach me that an illness couldn't take away from who I was and now I was left to suffer in silence. At least that's what they thought. But I decided to take my fate in my own hands.

Before I left this Earth, though, I needed to get some things off my chest.

"Honestly, Mr. Brown, I don't think it's a good idea. We need to keep you as germ free as possible." I started to protest but he quickly cut me off. "But—I understand your need. So I will have a nurse come wheel you down. But you have to keep it short. I nodded my head acknowledging what he had said. I didn't care what I had to agree to, as long as I got to spend some time with Money.

***

"I got it from here," I assured the petite nurse who wheeled me down to the floor Money was on.

"Well, here. Let me at least get you in the door," she offered with a genuine sound of concern in her voice.

"Just leave the door open and I can get myself in," I said in a husky tone. I could feel the tears well up in my eyes as soon I saw my homie laid out and so still. No matter what my condition was, I was a *man,* and no one would see me shed tears.

"Okay. I'm going to go down to the nurse's station. Just push the nurse's button when you're ready to go." I heard what she was saying, but I wouldn't be pushing that damn button. They'd have to come get me.

I waved her off as I wheeled closer to Money's bed. I sat for a few seconds watching the rise and fall of his chest. I knew he would be talking shit if he was awake, but I didn't even care. This was my nigga. We had been to the bottom and climbed our way to the top together.

I reached out and grabbed his hand as I felt the warm tears making streaks down my face. I would never let him see me cry and that was probably the only positive in the situation. He would have no idea I was letting the tears fall like I was some kind of female. "Money, bruh, we done been through a lot of shit together. We done sold drugs, bussed our guns and fucked hoes together. We always said we would die together and now look at us." I felt the authenticity of what I had just said and I couldn't stop myself from breaking down. I removed my hand from around Money's and covered my face. My body was rocked with the sobbing I was doing. I was 33 years old. I had no children and I was about to die. I never had a chance to fall in love, or travel outside of the country. I never got to name my first child. I didn't even own a fucking dog and there I was literally clinging to life.

I managed to half ass compose myself before I began speaking to my ace again. "Money, bruh. You gotta wake up. I haven't been able to watch over Schina as much as you would want because…" I wasn't ready to get into that yet, so I skipped the end of the sentence. "But boy, the times that I have seen her, she looked rough. It's bad enough she has went through all the drama behind the girls. But now this, too. I'm scared she's going to lose the baby. And boy…" I drifted off trying to picture the carnage that would lay at Dallas' feet.

"Bruh, there's something I need to tell you." There was no point in beating around the bush. I even let off a slight laugh as I heard his voice in my head. *Just get to the fucking point, Blue. Quit getting all emotional like a bitch and just say what the fuck you got to say, my nigga.*

"I hear you, dawg. Well, you already knew I have cancer. But what you ain't know was I had quit doing them damn injections. Man, that shit had me throwing up and all kinda shit dude. That shit wasn't made for gangstas like me." I was steady calling myself a gangsta, but the tears that continuously poured from my eyes spoke a whole other story. I wanted to knock the tears from my face, but I knew it would be futile. "Well nigga, to make a long story short, they've only given me two months to live. The cancer has spread too far out of control. There's nothing left to save me, G. And remember what I always told you would happen if it got to this point. Yea, you always said you wouldn't let me make that choice. But you can't interfere now, huh?"

I was overwhelmed with emotion as I stared at my boy. I hoped somehow he could hear me because what I was about to say was something he needed to take to heart.

The only noises in the room were the humming of the machines that sustained his life and the deep sniffles coming from my soul. My mind drifted back to the day Money and I met. A smile crept upon my tear stained face.

"Bruh, I know you ain't trying to hear me," I said as I took one of his hand into mine, "but I really hope you listen anyway. Bruh, Schina and those girls love you. I have never seen a woman look at a man the way that sis looks at you. She has put up with so much from you and still always manages to forgive you. As a matter of fact, bro, you have no one to blame for being here but yourself." I thought that I felt his hand jerk and I reflexively jumped. I stared at him for a few moments but didn't notice any other movement coming from his still body.

"Don't trip, my nigga. I'm just keeping it real with you. I know that you love her, too. I also know that if she really left you..." I trailed off because I honestly couldn't imagine how he would act. It was obvious from the situation at hand that he wouldn't be able to handle it well. "Well, I'm sure you would never find that level of happiness again. Ya know, out of all the bullshit we have been through, I have never asked you for anything. But today is that day, my nigga."

I knew if he was awake and well, I would never have gotten away with that conversation. He would have made some bum ass remark about minding my business. Like his business didn't always seem to find its way to my doorstep. I didn't even care at that moment, though, how mad he would have been. I needed to speak my peace. "Bruh, I need you to stop cheating on Schina. You have to do better. Look at me, nigga. I'm about to die having never experienced the love that you continuously take for granted. I'll never get the chance to propose. I'll never get the chance to say I do. Hell, I've never had a woman bust her guns for me. If you don't do anything else, Byron, I need you to do that for me. Cherish your life and those in it before it's too late." Just as I started crying uncontrollably, I felt Money squeeze my hand. The doctors had told us that his muscles and reflexes would make him do that, but I knew that was his way of agreeing to my favor. That was all I could take. I just lowered my head and let all of my emotions out, good and bad.

When I finally gathered enough composure to be able to lift my head again, I reached my hand in the pockets of the grey sweatpants I wore under the thin hospital gown. I let a satisfied smirk cross my face as I took in the gleam that sparkled off the edge of the brand new razor blades. I drug my eyes back to Money, before I started to speak again.

Chapter Thirty-One
Schina

I felt a huge lump in my chest as I stood quietly in the doorway, watching and listening to Blue as he poured his heart out to Money.

"I always told you if it ever got bad enough, I would take fate into my own hands. I always told you no moths fucka could tell me when I was gone go. That I would handle shit myself, and I guess that day has come."

My heart raced as I ducked behind the door jamb. I thought I had seen Blue's head turning in my direction. Regardless of what I had just witnessed, even though I knew what was about to happen, I wanted to give him his privacy.

I knew that Blue was about to slit his own wrists and I would let him. Even though Blue didn't know I was aware of his condition, I knew everything when it came to my crew. I also one about the conversation he was referring to. The night he had told Money hen would take his own life before he let a disease take him. I hadn't believed him back then, but I did respect his wishes.

I gathered myself and walked to the nearest elevator bank. I decided to go to the cafeteria and get something to eat and call Ivory and let her know what was going on. She wasn't one of my favorite people at that moment but she still was crew.

I was a ball of emotions and my hands were trembling as I pressed the button on the elevator. I was so torn. The mother in me wanted to grab a nurse and go stop Blue. The gangsta in me had to let him do what he felt he needed to do.

I knew one thing, for sure, though. There had been entirely too much going on over the last few months. I was drained. My ace was the one who put my husband in the coma, and as much as I wanted to just forgive her... I couldn't. I told her everything was good between us, but in all honesty, I was so angry. I couldn't stop the ugly thoughts from circling my head and that's why I spent so much time at Money's bedside. I simply didn't trust myself to be alone with her. My other best friend had turned out to be a conniving sack of shit and my husband was a vegetable. And if that wasn't enough stress, I had just walked away knowing my husband's right hand man was about to slit his wrists.

***

I was wrestling with my conscious as I sat in the front row at Blue's funeral. I had been going back and forth about whether I had done the right thing. Some of time I was sure that I had But then it would hit me not only had I walked away and allowed it, I let him do it in Money's hospital room. It was probably one of the few decisions I had made that I would question until my own dying day.

As I again let my mind wonder back to the day Blue had taken his life. I thought of the largest puddle of blood that had formed between Blue's legs. I pictured the smaller but darker puddle of blood that had formed in Money's bed. I saw how Blue was clutching Money's hand even in death. But then I envisioned how I had panicked. Not because Blue had actually gone through with it. No, I had panicked because I didn't want his blood contaminating my husband. I knew that he couldn't actually give Byron cancer like that. But of course I wasn't thinking rationally. I had gone screaming for a nurse like a crazy person. And I was feeling the guilt from that as well.

The fact that my husband wasn't there to send his brother to the other side was just another weight I was struggling to bear. I could tell that it was really bothering Ivory, too. The way her eyes kept darting between me and the casket was a dead giveaway. The thing was I really didn't give a fuck. She needed to feel as bad as me, if not worse. *It's her fault Money didn't get to say good bye to his best friend,* I thought irrationally.

I shook my head and tried to shake off the anger I was holding in. Deep inside, I knew she had done what she felt was necessary. He may very well have killed me that night, and I *definitely* would have done the same for her. But I needed to feel any other emotion besides sad and worried. Being angry was starting to feel good. I looked forward to the rush of heat that would wash over my body. I just hated that it was my best friend that I was feeling it towards.

"… Into ashes…" I knew the preacher was talking, probably going on and on about what a great person Blue was. But me, all I heard was the humming of the machines that were keeping my husband alive. Those machines that were in a room twenty-five miles away from the funeral home I sat in. I was devastated by the loss of Blue, but my mind and my heart were sitting in ICU. I kept getting this nagging feeling that I needed to be with Byron. *Fuck this*, I thought as I stood up causing all heads to turn my way. I'm sure they were expecting some kind of spectacle like last time, but even if Blue wasn't a stand up dude, my mind was elsewhere. I grabbed my purse and nodded my head at Ivory as I turned to rush out of the morbid funeral home.

Even though I was barely speaking to my best friend, I knew she knew where I was headed. I knew she would handle the rest of the service and the events that were scheduled for that evening. I had decided to send Blues ashes away in mini hot air balloons. There were six balloons being released that night. And the seventh one sat on my mantel, waiting for its rightful owner to heat it off and send it floating to the heavens. Ivory had mocked the ceremony, stating it was a little to Tyler Perryish for her taste. But I had no doubt she would make sure it went off smoothly. I also knew that she would pick up our daughters and play mommy and daddy to all three girls.

"I have to start spending more time at home. I cannot let this hospital become the headquarters of my life," I said out loud as

I steered my car through the early afternoon traffic. That's the words my mouth formed, but my heart knew better. As long as my husband needed me there to take care of him and make decisions, I was going to be there. Even though, in my heart, our relationship was truly over, I wasn't going to let anyone mistreat my husband. Not on my watch.

Yes, I had decided it was over no matter what became of his health. I was done with him hurting me and making me look stupid. I loved him, most days more than I loved myself. That's where the problems arose. Because I loved him so damn much I would settle for his bullshit. Not anymore, though. I was through. I couldn't let our daughters grow up thinking that being cheated on was normal or acceptable.

"But, Ima be here 'til you can take care of yourself," I said, gazing upwards as I pulled into the parking garage at the hoods trauma center, the very same center that had saved my own life. I meant every word that I said as I rushed to the entrance. I needed to be in his presence right then.

I hummed Teairra Mari's *Deserve* as I watched the numbers light up as the elevator neared Money's floor. I couldn't stop my foot from tapping and I was fighting not to bite my nails. I wasn't sure what was going on but I was more than anxious to get to Money. I just had a feeling that he needed me.

Finally, I thought as the doors gave off the last *ding,* letting me know I had reached my destination. I had just started to give a sigh of relief when I noticed a crowd of people rushing towards a room in the center of the hall. *Money's room,* I barely had time to think before I heard it. That mechanical voice that rudely shouts all medical emergencies.

Code Blue, Code Blue Room 1402.

It was like I felt my body give out. I had just been through too much and my body couldn't take another blow. I simultaneously felt the tears spew forward from my eyes and the intense cramping in my abdomen. I watched as the *pat, pat, pat* of blood spattering seemed to grow larger right in front of my eyes.

"Help. I'm pregnant." All I could do was hope that there was at least one nurse free to assist me.

"Ma'am, what's going on?" I heard the words coming from the older white woman's mouth. I just couldn't get my mouth to respond. "Someone get me a stretcher. We need to get her to Labor and Delivery."

"It's too early. They won't make it," I responded weakly, seconds before everything went black.

Epilogue
Schina
Two and a Half Years Later...

"Come here, Lil' Money," I said, calling my rambunctious two year old closer to me. He had gotten a little too close to the pool and it made me nervous.

"Wha, mama?" he asked as he ran closer to me.

As soon as he got within arm's reach, I swooped him up and tossed him in the air.

"Girl, put that grown ass man down. You know damn well you aren't supposed to be picking him up," Ivory said, pointing an accusing finger at my once again protruding belly.

"Girl, hush, weren't you just holding him ya damn self," I said nuzzling my nose into his curly tresses. I stared at him, trying to ignore Ivory. He was so gorgeous. He had skin the color of a paper bag and big bright eyes. He had his father's nose and lips but my hair. My baby had never had a haircut and his sandy brown hair hung to the middle of his back. I normally kept it braided, but I decided to leave it down today.

"Girl, ain't nobody ask you all that," she shot back as she finished hanging the last Mickey Mouse decoration and reached down and rubbed her own swollen belly. "Besides, you're further than me. It's more of a risk for you."

I sat my son back down on his feet and watched him scamper off to the bounce house in the corner of our backyard, before I threw her big bellied ass the middle finger. "Bitch, by two weeks."

We both laughed as we admired the decorations all over my backyard. Everything was red, yellow, or black and had a Mickey Mouse theme. My baby boy loved the hell out of that show and everyone knew in my eyes it was his world. Whatever it was that he wanted, I tried to make sure that he got. Ivory had once had the audacity to ask me if I spoiled him so much because of Kai'Shaun's death. I didn't think so, but I wouldn't swear to it either. All I knew was he was my young prince and I wanted to give him as much of the world as possible.

I had gone through so much stress while pregnant with him, it still amazed me that he was so healthy and intelligent. I knew all parents felt that their children were advanced, but even Byron Jr's pediatrician would express amazement at how smart my baby was.

"Mama," I heard the ever laughing voice of Tai. I turned and looked at my teenager. She had grown so much. She was still a tomboy, though. Today she was rocking a black t-shirt with Mickey Mouse in a typical gangster pose, some red capris, and her ever present J's. The ones she wore today, cuz Lord knows I couldn't tell them apart, were red white and black and had been airbrushed with her name in bright yellow. Of course her long beautiful hair had been tucked into a black Mickey Mouse hat. The back of her shirt as well as the matching shirt her sister was wearing were airbrushed across the back. They both said Birthday Boy's Sister. The only difference was Liv's shirt was fitted and paired with some red shorts and black sandals.

"Yes, my love?" I asked, pulling her in as close as I could against my eight month pregnant belly.

"Uh, there's some mice at the front door." She laughed as she pointed towards the house.

"I still can't believe your crazy ass hired fuc..." Ivory slapped her hand across her mouth. Even though my baby boy was clear on the other side of the yard, even she didn't want to spoil that surprise. He was going to be so excited.

"Yes, I hired Mickey and Minnie. I mean, my baby only turns two once, right?" I brushed her off as I began waddling towards the house. I needed to let them in and then shower and change into my outfit that matched my three children.

"I'll be back, Ivory. You got the kids for about thirty minutes, right?"

"Kids, bitch bye. The only kid out here is Lil' Money. Tai and Liv are grown ass women. They ain't gone do shit but play on them damn tablets."

I laughed because right as she said that Liv slipped her sandals off and dived into the giant ball pit that sat catty corner to the bounce house. There was so much stuff to do in the backyard, I just didn't agree.

"Just keep my kids safe while I stash the mice and shower. I'll put your outfit on the bed in the room you slept in last night, cool?"

She just waved me off as I resumed my waddle into my new nine thousand square foot house. It was an apology gift from Jorge, and even though I accepted the gift and the apology, and even though the crew still rocked with the cartel, I had never spoken to him again. The bastard had shot me while I was pregnant. How do you hold a civil conversation with someone after that? I often asked myself.

I had to admit it was a hell of an apology gift, though. The six bedrooms would be put to good use considering I was about to go from proud mom of three to overwhelmed mother of five. Hell, I still wasn't sure if four bathrooms was enough, and that's why I had been keeping my eyes open for something bigger. I appreciated the family room, media room, gym, and all the other things that this house offered, but I had to consider I was going to have three girls vying for bathroom space at some time in the future. Times were going to get rough and I was trying to be proactive.

I was snapped out of my thinking by Tai grabbing my hand. "Are you okay, mama," she asked with her voice full of concern. She had been so attentive throughout this pregnancy. I absolutely loved the way our relationship had flourished.

"Yea, baby, I'm okay. I was just wondering if we should move."

"Why, mama?" This time her voice was high pitched and sad sounding. The girls absolutely loved this house. Being surrounded by trees, I had separate cottages built "in the woods" as the girls called it. Each cottage had separate themes. There was a makeover cottage, a snack cottage, a sports viewing cottage, a video game cottage, and a couple more. The girls loved to get on their four-wheelers and cruise out there and do whatever it is they did.

I remember when I first had them built. Ivory talked so much shit I had to hang up on her. "They're going to be out there having sex. They're going to smoke weed. Tai is going to ruin her sports career." Blah blah blah.

No one knew my kids as well as me and that just wasn't a concern I had at that point. Not to mention, there was no way they were getting any boys passed the tight ass security that monitored our house 24/7. I was taking no risks with my family's safety. I had learned that lesson the hard way.

I laughed before I responded to my first born. "Don't worry, babe." I ruffled her hair, which I knew she hated. "If we move, we will take your little houses. I just think with the twins coming, eventually we will need more room."

I watched as she attempted to smooth her hair back down, and seemed to think about my answer. "Yea, that might be true, mama. But what you gonna do about Mickey and them?" I had completely forgotten about the Disney characters I had rented for the duration of Byron Jr's party. "I left them sitting on the benches in the front hall."

"Okay, my love. I will go get them as comfortable as I can get them until it's time for them to show their faces. Do me a favor, you, Liv, and Danyelle," I said speaking of Ivory's daughter, "go play in the backyard. Help Ivory's big belly ass keep your brother out of the house. I don't want him running up on his surprise."

"We got you, mama," she agreed, as she ran off to get her lifelong best friend. Both of the girls loved Byron Jr just as much as I did. They never complained about having to help with him. I laughed as I remembered how when he was a baby, I had to make a baby sign out sheet for his room. The girls were always sneaking in there and taking him to their rooms. I would get all hysterical, thinking someone had stolen my baby. This went on for weeks before I made the sheets. When they would take him out of his room, they would literally have to sign him out, almost like at daycare.

I continued my trek to the front hall and laughed as I saw Mickey, Minnie, Donald, and Daisy lounging around. "Hey, everyone. Y'all are way early and I appreciate that, but I have to figure out what to do with y'all."

"Well, I can help them out of their costumes until it's time if that would make it easier," a baritone voice said. I looked around but didn't see anyone, until *he* stood up. He had been hidden by the bulky bodies of the characters.

I gasped as I felt the twins kicking, both of them at one time. It was almost like they were trying to remind me of who and where the hell I was. An almost nine month pregnant mother of almost five, who damn sure didn't need those kind of problems.

Even being brought back to my reality, I couldn't help but to appreciate the sight before me. The kids and I had gone back to Disney last year and I could not remember seeing a character handler like the one that stood before me. He had to be six feet two inches and around two hundred fifty pounds of pure muscle. With skin the color of melted chocolate, eyes the color of honey, and wavy hair, he had my full attention. When he spoke again with that Barry White voice, I almost had to cross my legs. "Hi, I'm Montavion. I will be your characters assistant today."

"Hi, I'm, uh, I'm Schina. I'm the mom of the birthday boy." I reached out to shake his extended hand. It was like touching pure silk.

"Yes, I figured as much," he laughed. His teeth were even perfect. Again I grimaced as the twins started acting up. "Are you okay, ma'am?" He was eyeing my stomach and trying to lead me to the bench where the characters were still sitting patiently. I thought of how uncomfortable they must be and shook my head.

"No, I'm good. The babies are just super active right now," I explained. "But, yes, let me show y'all to the media room where you can get them out of those costumes and more comfortable. You all can watch a movie or something until it's time for them to come out. There's drinks and snacks down there, too," I explained as I started leading through my house. I was walking as fast as my belly would allow. I not only was running out of time before the party started, I needed to get away from Mr. Montavion.

***

Ivory and I were showered and in our outfits greeting children and parents as I was trying to tell her all about the goody stashed in my media room. "Girl, he is…"

"Going to wind up missing if my wife don't watch it," I heard my husband's voice. While he was laughing, I knew he was so serious.

"Awww, boo, you know your wife doesn't want anyone but you." I turned around and stared into the eyes of the father of my youngest four children and my husband of thirteen years.

Yes, Money and I stayed together. Once, he recovered from the bullet Ivory put in his back, he turned over a whole new leaf. It was like the things Blue had said to him that night really got to him.

He had become such a good man. I could honestly say I had no worries on where he was sticking his dick. I always knew where he was. Even running the crew, he was always home at a decent hour, and if he was going to be late, he made sure to call home and let me know. I had gotten back the same man I had fallen in love with all those years ago.

There were nights I heard him crying quietly over Blue's death. What seemed to make his pain deeper was the fact that he hadn't been able to attend Blue's funeral. I knew that no words I could utter would erase his grief. I wished I could take that pain away from him, but I knew I couldn't. I thought I had prepared myself for that, but I honestly had no idea how bad it was going to hit him. I would just hold him on the real bad nights, there was nothing else I could offer.

Ivory punched Money in the arm, and I took a moment to appreciate the fact that they got along so well now. They had actually made up and forgiven each other before I forgave either one of them. It was like once she shot him, all of her aggravation and disdain for him disappeared. Whatever, it was all in the past. "Shut up, bruh. You know damn well her fat ass loves only you. Now where the hell you leave my husband," she asked speaking of Chris' big swole body ass. I loved that they had finally hooked up and gotten married. He loved Ivory more than he loved life itself and Danyelle was rather fond of him as well. Now that she was expecting their first child, he had made her leave the streets alone, too. Now him and Money ran the crew and shit was going pretty well. I don't know if it was because our men had really stepped up their game, or if it was because the streets knew how I gave it up. And they knew after all these years, through all the drama, I Still Ride For My Hitta.

The End

Coming Soon from Lock Down Publications/Ca$h Presents

TORN BETWEEN TWO

By **Coffee**

LAST OF A DYING BREED

LAY IT DOWN **III**

By **Jamaica**

BLOOD OF A BOSS **IV**

By **Askari**

BRIDE OF A HUSTLA **III**

By **Destiny Skai**

WHEN A GOOD GIRL GOES BAD **II**

By **Adrienne**

LOVE & CHASIN' PAPER **II**

By **Qay Crockett**

THE HEART OF A GANGSTA **II**

By **Jerry Jackson**

Available Now

RESTRAING ORDER **I & II**

By **CA$H & Coffee**

LOVE KNOWS NO BOUNDARIES **I II & III**

By **Coffee**

LAY IT DOWN **I & II**

By **Jamaica**

PUSH IT TO THE LIMIT

By **Bre' Hayes**

BLOOD OF A BOSS **I II & III**

By **Askari**

THE STREETS BLEED MURDER **I, II & III**

THE HEART OF A GANGSTA

By **Jerry Jackson**

CUM FOR ME

An **LDP Erotica Collaboration**

BRIDE OF A HUSTLA **I II**

By **Destiny Skai**

WHEN A GOOD GIRL GOES BAD

By **Adrienne**

A GANGSTER'S REVENGE **I II III & IV**

By **Aryanna**

WHAT ABOUT US **I & II**

NEVER LOVE AGAIN

THUG ADDICTION

By **Kim Kaye**

THE KING CARTEL **I, II & III**

By **Frank Gresham**

THESE NIGGAS AIN'T LOYAL **I, II & III**

By **Nikki Tee**

GANGSTA SHYT **I II &II**I

By **CATO**

THE ULTIMATE BETRAYAL

By **Phoenix**

DON'T FU#K WITH MY HEART **I & II**

By **Linnea**

BOSS'N UP **I & II**

By **Royal Nicole**

I LOVE YOU TO DEATH

By Destiny J

I RIDE FOR MY HITTA

By **Misty Holt**

LOVE & CHASIN' PAPER

By **Qay Crockett**

<u>BOOKS BY LDP'S CEO, CA$H</u>

TRUST NO MAN

TRUST NO MAN 2

TRUST NO MAN 3

BONDED BY BLOOD

SHORTY GOT A THUG

A DIRTY SOUTH LOVE

THUGS CRY

THUGS CRY 2

TRUST NO BITCH

TRUST NO BITCH 2

TRUST NO BITCH 3

TIL MY CASKET DROPS

RESTRAINING ORDER

RESTRAINING ORDER 2

<u>Coming Soon</u>

TRUST NO BITCH (KIAM EYEZ' STORY)

THUGS CRY 3

BONDED BY BLOOD 2

IN LOVE WITH HIS GANGSTA

Stay Connected with Us!

Text **LOCKDOWN** to 22828 to stay up-to-date with new releases, sneak peaks, contests and more…